NINE DAYS IN MILAN
A NICK THOMAS ADVENTURE

PATRICK LIVANOS LESTER

Nine Days in Milan/Patrick Lester—1st ed. 1.5

Book cover art and design by Patrick Lester

Print ISBN: 978-1-948992-08-4

Digital ISBN: 978-1-948992-09-1

For Kim, my partner in love, adventure, and life.

Thanks to my editors and beta readers Ruth McDonnell, Genie Lester, Sandy Boucher, Debra Alderson, and Milton Palmer. Special thanks to Fernando Colombres for introducing me to Horatio, whose services I hope I will never need.

In Memory of Ruth McDonnell, editor extraordinaire and a source of great encouragement.

Troppo di Questo è Vero
(Too Much of This is True)

PART ONE

HONOLULU

ONE
A RITE OF PASSAGE

Honolulu's hot, muggy September air hung heavy as Nick Thomas sat shaded by the dodger of his sailboat and home, Icarus. The boat had been handed down from his grandfather to his father, and then to him. Looking out at the Ala Wai Boat Harbor, Nick saw people were moving lethargically and flags were limp. His clothes were soaked through with perspiration. He took a healthy swallow of water from his flask and was about to go below and into the air-conditioned cabin when his phone rang.

He checked the caller ID and answered, "Good morning, Willie."

"Hey, Nick. A woman on the windward side needs help with her modeling agency. You're always up for the new and exciting."

"Exciting. Right. I don't mean to sound ungrateful, but I might remind you I still have the mark from the last client you recommended me to." Nick touched his side and felt the scar from the bullet that had torn through his flesh and lodged in the companionway trim on Icarus.

"Call it a dueling scar—a rite of passage," Willie said. "Anyway, I met her at a party on the beach. We got talking. She needed help, and I thought of you."

"Thanks, Willie. Please give her my number and have her give me a call," Nick said.

"Yeah, I already did. I've got to go. Tell me later how it works out."

Willie hung up. Nick looked at his telephone.

"A rite of passage?"

Two

Suzanne Langston

The next day Nick's phone rang as he unlocked the hatch on Icarus. He climbed down the stairs and into the saloon.

"This is Nick," he said, answering the phone and dropping onto the settee.

"Hello, this is Suzanne Langston. William Lee suggested I talk to you about the help I need with my business." The voice was professional, calm, collected.

"Willie said I was to expect a call. What can I do for you?"

Nick reached for the notepad and pen on the table.

"I own a modeling agency. An Italian company asked me to team with them to expand their business opportunities for modeling and model production in Hawaii. They want to put in a production facility, model training facility, and a model camp to house the models when they are here on photoshoots. I need help, and William told me you were the one to call."

"Perhaps we should meet and discuss the details," Nick said.

"Do you know *Aquamarine*?"

"The restaurant downtown?"

"Can we meet there Wednesday at twelve for lunch?" she asked.

Nick thought of his schedule. "I can be there at noon on Wednesday."

"Great. See you then."

On Wednesday, Nick dressed in Hawaii business attire of trousers and a pressed aloha shirt with a subtle pattern of ukuleles and sailboats. He drove in his vintage black Triumph convertible past Ala Moana Center, the beach park, the cruise ship terminals, and Aloha Tower, then made a right turn away from the tourists and into the business district. The restaurant *Aquamarine* was in a converted Chinatown storefront on the edge of downtown Honolulu. It was one of the finer restaurants on the island.

Nick found a parking spot, entered the restaurant, and surveyed the scene. The place had high ceilings and hardwood floors; the walls were indigo blue. Designed with an Indo-European motif, the tables and chairs were of intricate hand-carved wood. The tables had white tablecloths and were set with fine dishes and cutlery. The cooled air was refreshing after the warm trip in his Triumph.

The *maître d'* approached.

"Mr. Thomas?" The guy had his nose in the air and a twisted mouth. He had a bored look on his face.

"Yes, that's me." *Was this guy for real?*

"Follow me, please." He slithered off in an eastward direction. Nick followed, and they passed a woman playing classical music on a baby grand piano before he was deposited at a table. The woman before him was coifed and immaculately turned out in a taupe number. *Polished—a rare sight in the islands.*

"Nicholas John Thomas," he said, extending his hand.

"Suzanne Langston." Her grip exuded confidence. "Thanks for coming. William said you could help me. Shall we have a bite of lunch before we launch into business?"

"Good idea," Nick said, picking up the menu.

They ordered dim sum appetizers of pumpkin rolls and ahi sashimi with avocado slices. It was an odd mixture and exquisite to the palate. Nick assumed the ahi was caught the day before, the taste clean and fresh, the texture firm and smooth and accented by the sharp and gritty taste of the wasabi and soy sauce. Between bites, Suzanne described her business and what it currently entailed.

She had been in Hawaii for some twenty years and had a modeling agency for most of that time. Her client list was vast and impressive, including most of the major fashion houses. Her models appeared in magazines, catalogs, and television commercials all over the world.

With the food finished, they ordered espresso and the conversation turned to business.

"The upshot is an Italian modeling agency owner wants to expand his business. The man I've been talking to is Luigi Donati. He was in Honolulu last month to meet with me," she said, taking lipstick from her purse and applying it.

"The name of his agency is *swank*. The logo is with lowercase letters in italics."

"*swank* models?" Nick asked.

Suzanne shrugged. "I suggested they find a better name before they get too much attention. Anyway, I have a good reputation in the industry for finding new talent. They want me to manage the process and go to Milan to discuss the deal with them. It's out of my comfort range—the business aspects, that is—and I want to make sure I get the best deal possible." She reached for her espresso.

Nick took a sip of espresso, giving him time to consider the prospect. He set down his cup. "Business negotiations can be difficult. I like to put my cards on the table, but you can't expect others to do the same. Throw in a cross-cultural element, and who knows what is really going on? It would be best to decide in advance what you want out of it."

"They want me to put together and run the whole thing."

"Is it something you'd like to do?"

"It would change my focus a great deal. I guess it depends on how the company is structured."

"How well do you know this Luigi?"

"I met him for the first time when he was here last month. He was throwing around a lot of cash and made sure I saw his stack of $100 bills," Suzanne replied. "He wants me to go to Milan to discuss the project."

"It would be a good idea to do due diligence on Mr. Donati. Ask around the industry and find out about him," Nick said.

"There are a couple of people I can reach out to."

"What would you like me to do for you?" He reached for his water glass.

"I need a draft agreement to give to Luigi."

"When do you leave?"

"A couple of weeks? I need to make a budget. Luigi said he would send me a first-class ticket, pay my expenses, and cover the cost of lost revenue from my business while I'm abroad."

"I must caution you not to leave until you get the money upfront, or at least a good portion of it." Nick took another sip of espresso. "Make sure the cheque clears the bank before you head to the airport. As for the negotiations, that could be tough. What's the time difference, twelve hours?"

"Eleven."

"Are you interested in helping me with this?" Suzanne asked.

"I can help with the budget and the draft agreement. Then we can send it to an attorney to formalize it. We would need to find a competent lawyer skilled in international law. I can recommend a California firm. I don't know of one in Hawaii, but I could ask around."

"How do we proceed?" Suzanne asked.

"I'll send you a consulting contract this afternoon. It will be for a set number of hours and you can cancel it at any time and pay me for what I've done."

"That sounds fair enough."

"I suppose you could email, call, or text me daily about what is going on once you're in Italy. I could review any agreement you and Luigi make and get back to you. One misses a lot of the nuances of doing it that way. I'm not sure how much I can do to help you without being there."

"I could see how that would be a problem. You should probably come with me to Milan. Would that be possible?"

Nick considered it for a moment. There was a lull in his consulting while one of his clients secured funding.

"That would probably be the most effective arrangement," Nick agreed.

"These people have a lot of money, and I could work your expenses into my fees," Suzanne said.

"Let's put together a budget and see how the numbers come out." They finished their drinks and headed their separate ways.

Nick and Suzanne spent the week talking on the phone and emailing each other's budget numbers back and forth. Nick wrote a budget proposal, and Suzanne sent it to Luigi for review. It was slow going, with the time difference and Luigi's delayed responses to her queries.

It was nearing midnight in Milan and Luigi Donati sat on the sofa in his apartment and plotted his next move. The time change made it easier for him to elude Suzanne Langston's questions and requests for the money.

He had been planning for months, perhaps years, waiting for

the perfect opportunity. Suzanne Langston was the ideal start. She was far away in Hawaii but still in the United States. She had a respected business with a well-known international clientele.

He looked at his mobile phone.

Now, what will he do about the business associate she is planning to bring with her?

Three

I hate to drink alone

Two years before in San Francisco, Lance Grabowski, Nick's friend and business partner, embezzled more than $32 million from Nick and their investors, then vanished into the wind. Nick was left nearly penniless from the crime. He only still had Icarus because his friends had chipped in and bought it from Nick's creditors.

Nick continued with the unending maintenance on Icarus while waiting for Suzanne to finalize details with Luigi. He spent the afternoon disassembling the main sheet winch, cleaning it, and repacking it with grease.

It had turned into a sultry evening. Nick had finished eating dinner and was standing on the stern watching the sunset reflecting off the windows of the Marina Tower in Waikiki. He could hear the DJ at a hotel playing the current hit songs, and a laugh or splash from the swimming pool. Moving to the stereo, he turned it up. In the spirt of his upcoming Italian trip, he exchanged the Hawaiian music he usually played for an Italian opera. That evening's selection was *Tosca* by Puccini.

Nick peered over the side of the boat. A pufferfish had taken to showing up around sunset, and Nick often fed it scraps of his dinner. The fish saw him and came to the surface, its enormous eyes questioning Nick.

"Nothing for you tonight, George."

The fish regarded him for a moment, then turned away.

Nick was about to drop into a beanbag chair in the cockpit when his mobile phone rang. It was Nigel, an Englishman friend of Nick and Willie, and a fellow sailor.

"Hey Nick, I'm at the gate."

"I'll be right there."

Nick walked down the dock to let Nigel in and followed him back to the boat. As they approached the stern, a six-inch-long centipede crawled up from between the dock boards.

"Aiii!" Nigel yelled, took off his slipper, and nudged the centipede into the water. "I hate those things. The last time one grabbed me it hurt for days."

Nick and Nigel looked over the dock and into the water. George, the pufferfish, shot out from under the stern of Icarus and bit the centipede in two.

"Nice going, George," Nigel said.

Sitting in the cockpit back on Icarus, Nigel opened his backpack and pulled out a bottle of whisky and two glasses. "I hate to drink alone," he said, pouring two fingers of whiskey into each glass.

"I'm ready to haul out the *Lizard* and scrape the hull and do other work on her," Nigel said. He lived nearby onboard *Awkward Lizard*, a fifty-one-foot coastal cruiser.

"The joys of boat ownership," Nick said, taking a sip of whisky and letting out a cough. "What is this stuff?"

"*Laphroaig*. Islay single malt scotch."

"It smells and tastes like a peat bog."

"It's an acquired taste."

"I'll say. Hey, if my Milan trip pans out, would you like to stay on Icarus while I'm gone and Awkward Lizard is hauled out? It's tight quarters compared to the mansion you live on, but it has air conditioning. You can use my car, too."

"Hey, that would be great. I was going to get a hotel. This will save me at least a thousand dollars."

A slight and welcome breeze came across the harbor and the sky took on the hues of sunset.

They sat quietly and sipped their drinks.

Nigel ran his fingertip across a patched hole in the molding around the companionway. "Is this where you had that spot of bother?"

"Spot of bother? You guys sure downplay me being shot. Yes, that's where the bullet ended up after it went through me."

Nigel leaned forward and inspected the flaw in the wood.

"Willie called it 'a rite of passage'," Nick said.

"That sounds like Willie."

Four

Full moon party

"Hello," he shouted into his mobile phone attached to the dashboard, "Nick here."

"Nick?"

"Yes, that's me."

"Where are you?" It was Suzanne.

"I'm driving on H1. I need to pull over so we can talk." He down-shifted and slammed on the brakes to avoid a Ford Mustang convertible pulling into his lane with nary a glance. The barcode on the back window showed it to be a rental car. Nick turned off at the next exit, took Kīlauea Avenue to Kāhala Mall, and parked in the lot.

He took the phone from its mount. "Okay, I'm back."

"It sounds like you're in an airplane–that's flying underwater."

"It's this wonderful digital cellular technology. You should hear what it sounds like with the top down on my car."

"Why do they test market this technology stuff in Hawaii?"

"We are so far from anyone else, if it's truly awful, no one hears of it."

"That makes sense."

"What can I do for you?" Nick asked.

"I'm having a full moon party this Friday. It's kind of a reoccurring event."

"The full moon or the party?" he asked.

"Both." He could almost hear her roll her eyes. "Can you make it?"

"Yes, thank you for the invitation. What can I bring?"

"How about something to drink?"

"Sure. What time?"

"Sunset."

"I'll be there."

It was approaching sunset on Friday evening. Nick had the top down on his Triumph and was heading through east Honolulu, past Hawaii Kai, Sandy Beach, Makapu'u Lighthouse, and on to Waimānalo. The car ran well and Nick found the drive to be one of the most pleasurable on the island. The sunset, the note of exhaust, and the jazz on the stereo made it perfect. Two bottles of champagne were in an ice chest on the passenger seat. He wore shorts and slippers and his father's vintage aloha shirt with hula girls and flying fish. He turned right on a side street lined with limousines, drove toward the ocean, idled down the lane, and parked. The clock on the dashboard read 7:45; he would be early by Hawaiian standards. He took the bottles from the cooler, put the top up, and headed to the house. A note on the gate read, "We're at the beach." The path was lined with tiki torches, and he made his way past the mangrove and spiky kiawe toward the music.

He came upon a party in full force. There was a band, a bonfire, and tables set up overflowing with food. A horse trough was filled with ice and liquid refreshments. He found Suzanne serving food at one table.

"Oh, Bollinger. Very nice." She took the bottles and slid them deep into the trough.

"Those need to settle down before they're opened," Nick said.

"Everyone, this is Nick," Suzanne introduced.

"Hi, Nick," greeted the crowd.

Nick waved to the throng.

"Nick," came a voice from the crowd.

It was Willie.

Standing by himself in the shallow surf, Willie felt the waves lapping over his feet. The sun was setting behind the *Pali* and the tips of the waves were lit up in oranges and reds.

Nick walked down to the water to join him.

"What are you doing here?"

Willie looked down at the sand and kicked a small pile. "Helena and I broke up and Suzanne invited me to her party. So here I am, adrift."

Nick had seen it coming for a while. There was nothing to do but watch and be there for his friend when it happened.

"I'm sorry, Willie. I like Helena," Nick said.

"Yeah, I like her too."

Willie viewed most of his relationships with women as temporary. Helena, however, had reached into Willie's soul and grabbed hold. But it didn't go both ways. There are few experiences as painful as letting yourself fall for someone and realizing they're standing above you, looking down at you.

"What are you doing tomorrow?" Nick asked.

"I was going to spend the day with Helena. Now that isn't going to happen. I'm not sure what I'm going to do."

"Stay here. I'll go get us a couple of drinks and we can talk about it," Nick said.

"Okay."

On the way back to the drinks table, Nick pulled his mobile phone from his pocket and made a call.

"Are you still one crew short for the race tomorrow?" Nick asked.

"Yeah, we are," Bligh replied. His crew referred to the owner and skipper of the boat as Bligh, but not to his face. He used what Nick referred to as the 1700s British Naval model of leadership. He yelled a lot. But he was a fine helmsman and kept his boat in excellent condition.

"My friend Willie is free to crew," Nick said.

"You're talking about the guy we picked up when he fell overboard at the mark last year?" Bligh asked. "He nearly got run over by a dozen boats before we got to him."

"He's a fine sailor and has a boat of his own. He knows what he's doing," Nick said.

"I haven't found anyone else. I guess he'll be okay."

"Great. We will meet you tomorrow morning at the dock," Nick said.

"Let's hope he can stay onboard this time."

Nick grabbed a bottle of beer for Willie and a glass of champagne for himself.

Willie was still standing in the surf facing the Island of Molokai and the lights on the island's western shore.

Nick handed him the beer. "Bligh needs another crew for the state championships tomorrow morning."

"Oh, yeah?"

"I enlisted you," Nick said. "We're going to have an early night. The gun goes off at nine a.m. You can stay with me on Icarus tonight so you don't have to drive over the hill early in the morning."

"Who else is crewing?"

"Nigel."

"Of course. I forgot he crewed with you. Every boat needs a crazy foredeck Englishman. But tell me, do you actually like this sailboat racing stuff?" Willie asked, taking a sip of beer.

"I race to sail, I don't sail to race," Nick said. "And it's a lot easier than taking my house out of the dock."

It was a much later night than Nick expected. Shortly after sunset, fireworks were shot over the water and the band kicked in. Before the party ended, there were belly dancers, a juggler, an improvisational dance performance, people riding horses through the surf, and a lot of skinny-dipping in the ocean.

Willie was quite taken with one of the belly dancers.

Five

Bad Latitude

The crew—Bligh, Nick, Willie, and Nigel—assembled on the dock at the Waikiki Yacht Club the next morning.

Bligh eyed the book in Willie's hand, *Our Man in Havana* by Graham Greene. "Plan on catching up on your reading during the race?" he asked.

"You never know," Willie said.

They emptied Bligh's boat, *Bad Latitude*, of unnecessary weight, including bunk cushions, unneeded equipment, and the all-important blender for making boat drinks when they got back to the dock.

The boat didn't have an engine and they sailed to the starting mark practicing tacking drills on the way. By the time they approached the mark, they had tacked and jibed half a dozen times and fallen into a good rhythm.

Bligh was in his customary mode of shouting orders during the drills.

"Doesn't this guy ever let up?" Willie asked Nick.

"Not really," Nigel said, coming back to the cockpit.

"How long before the start?" Willie asked.

Nick checked his watch. "Eight minutes."

"I have to use the bathroom," Willie said, heading below.

"On a boat, it's called 'the head'," Bligh shouted after him.

Later, during the final leg of the race, Willie asked Nick to give him a hand with a 'rope'.

"There are no 'ropes' on a boat. They are 'lines', or if they control sails, 'sheets,'" Bligh yelled.

A sailboat was on its way downwind from Maui to Honolulu when the race got underway. *Raison d'être* had arrived from California in late July with the Transpac—The Transpacific Yacht Race. The father-daughter crew had since been touring the islands.

"The racers are out today," the daughter said, turning the wheel to avoid sailing through the course.

The father took the binoculars hanging from the compass binnacle and watched the sailboats racing toward the windward mark. "I was never much of a racer, but these crews are good," he said.

"I wish I could stay and sail south with you, but I need to get back to California and school. University starts next week. I'll stick around until then and help you provision the boat and clean the hull. When does your crew arrive? I'd like to meet them before I go."

"They are already on the island. They're a couple of Kiwi sisters making their way home," the father said.

"Sisters? It should be like old times for you, like Beatrix and me growing up on this tub."

"That came out when we met and interviewed each other. They said they would love to meet you. We have dinner with them tomorrow."

The starting gun went off, and a couple of hours later, *Bad Latitude* was running with the two other boats at the front of the pack.

"Nick, how are we doing?" Bligh asked.

Nick gave a quarter turn on the jib sheet before answering.

"Usually, the boat to watch is the women's team on *Hecate*. They're a great crew, but they had a rudder problem at the start. We're pretty far ahead of them."

"So, how are we doing?" Bligh demanded.

"We're doing fine. Just pay attention to your driving. I'll do the rest."

Nigel usually worked the foredeck, but now he and Willie acted as ballast, moving around to keep the boat level for the best speed.

Nick scanned the horizon and monitored the other boats. He saw a wind line ahead.

"Nick," Bligh called.

"I see it."

"Is it a header or puff?"

"I can't tell yet."

Nick tried to gauge if the wind would hit the boat head-on or from the side. Either way, they would have to adjust the boat accordingly—and quickly to stay competitive. He watched *Broken Compass*, the boat in front of them, enter the wind line.

"Their sails are beginning to flap," Willie said.

"It's called *luffing,*" Bligh said.

Nick looked up at the mainsail. "It's a header. Get ready to turn to port. Willie and Nigel, get ready to move."

"Ready," they called.

Bligh turned the boat. "Ease, ease," he yelled.

Their speed picked up and *Broken Compass* slowed down.

"We can slide behind them and overtake them now," Nick said.

Bligh worked with the crew to pass the other boat and place themselves even with *Daft Griffin*, a group of expatriate Brits renowned for hard racing and even harder drinking.

They settled into the course, Nick making minor adjustments to the sails and asking Willie and Nigel to move to the starboard rail. He kept an eye on the finish line between the bright yellow pyramid-shaped inflated buoy serving as the final mark and the committee boat. He glanced at *Daft Griffin*; *Bad Latitude* was running even with the Brits.

"Give me something, Nick," Bligh said. It was the first time he hadn't shouted all day.

"Hold your course." Nick checked the jib and main sails. He had made the adjustments he could, and they were pulling every bit of speed out of the boat. "Nobody move. We are perfectly tuned."

"But *Daft* is right with us. How are we going to beat them?" Bligh asked, still not shouting.

Nick checked their competitors. They, too, were finely tuned.

Then one of the crew in a neon green T-shirt who had been sitting on the companionway hatch got up and moved to the back of the boat.

"Nick," Bligh hissed. "Give me something."

"Hold your course. We got a break. Check out their boat."

The crew looked at *Daft Griffin*. The guy in neon green had unzipped and was relieving himself off the back of the boat.

"What a way to lose a race. What an idiot," Nigel said.

"I don't get it," Willie said.

"With boats this light, even 150 pounds moved to the stern will slow them down a lot. My countrymen should have gone light on the beer before the race," Nigel explained.

Sure enough, *Bad Latitude* eased away from *Daft Griffin*.

They were a full two boat lengths ahead when they were the first to cross the finish line.

While sailing back to the dock, Willie dropped below and came back to the cockpit with the bowline.

"I'm going up to the pointy end and get us a ride back," Willie announced.

"Pointy end? It's called the bow. Now you're just messing with me," Bligh said.

"Bligh takes himself too seriously," Willie said to Nick as he passed.

Willie stood on the bow and hailed the committee boat to secure a tow back to the yacht club while Nick and Nigel took down the sails and bagged and stowed them.

Back at the dock, Nick came topside to find the blender whirling. Willie was holding cups for Bligh to fill when the blender stopped.

Sitting on the bow with Nick, Willie took a sip. "One thing you can say about Bligh, he makes a terrific blended boat drink, which is rarely light on the rum."

An hour later, the blender had stopped whirring, and the crew sat quietly on the boat. They would receive their trophy at a ceremony the following week.

Willie sat back, let out a belch, and turned to Nick.

"I'm hungry."

"Are you guys up for sushi? You did a great job today. I'm buying," Bligh said.

"Sushi sounds great. Where do you have in mind?" Nick asked.

"I'm thinking *Kats* would be a good choice," Bligh replied.

Nick and Nigel met eyes, then turned to Willie.

"*Kats Sushi*? The all-you-can-eat sushi place? I'll drive," Willie said.

They piled into Willie's huge white 1980s Cadillac and he started the car. The stereo came on with the engine.

"What is this heavy metal we are listening to?" Bligh asked.

Willie leaned forward and turned down the music.

"Béla Bartók. The original headbanger," Willie said.

Bligh glanced down. "What the hell? I can see the street under the floorboards."

"Yeah, I should fix that one of these days," Willie said.

Twenty minutes later, they were sitting at a well-worn wooden table in *Kats* on King Street on the edge of the business district. The restaurant mostly catered to the downtown office crowd of business people and government employees.

Willie studied the menu intently. The menu had rules regarding the all-you-can-eat service: finish everything, including all rice before ordering more, don't waste; you will be charged for leftovers.

Willie finished reading the rules, leaned back, and cracked his knuckles.

An hour and a half later, they were in Willie's car and heading back to the yacht club.

"You really outdid yourself, Willie," Nick said.

"I can't believe you got banned for life," Bligh said.

"He told me if you didn't stop eating, he would go bankrupt and have to close his shop," Nick said.

"Did you catch those photos on the wall on the way in? Those guys were also banned—and they are all sumo wrestlers," Nigel added.

"I may have actually eaten too much," Willie said, tapping his chest with his fist and belching.

"You're kidding," Nick said.

"I'm glad I was here to hear it myself, or I wouldn't have believed it," Nigel added.

Willie turned onto Ala Moana Boulevard. "Hey, do you think if I brought him a photo of me he would put it up with the banned sumo wrestlers?"

Six

A huge south shore swell was winding down. It had started a few days before, pounding the coast from Ka'ena Point on Oahu's northwest shore around the airport and Waikiki to beyond Diamond Head. Waikiki received the brunt of it, with waves approaching twenty feet. The rest of the islands were feeling it as well; Maui and the Big Island had waves breaking over rooftops and sweeping clean an oceanside wedding.

Nick had spent the weekend watching over Icarus and peering through his binoculars at the extreme surfers taking advantage of the big surf. The weather had changed in Hawaii like everywhere else. It was hotter in the summer and the storms were more intense.

He watched the waves breaking over the seawalls and pondered how the waterfront homes were faring and what their absentee owners were now thinking of their purchases. If it weren't for the reefs, there would be a lot more damage. As it was, the state lifeguards were kept busy, rescuing tourists and locals alike.

Now, with the relative calm from the subsiding surf, Nick

decided it was time to get out of Waikiki for the day. He was rest-less and his car needed a long drive.

He changed into swim shorts, slathered on sunscreen, put on a long sleeve t-shirt for added sun protection, filled a flask with water, and put it into his old leather daypack with an apple and an orange. He added his sketchbook and pencil case, then took an *Outrigger Canoe Club* cap off the shelf in the saloon and headed to his car.

The weather bringing the big surf had cooled the island, and the trade winds were a comfortable ten knots. Nick unlatched the convertible top and slid into the driver's seat. Leaving the noise and chaos of Waikiki behind, he drove past Ala Moana Center to Piʻikoi Street and on to H1, continuing past Pearl Harbor, and through Mililani in the middle of the island. Traffic was sparse on Sunday morning. He passed Dole Plantation, once a producer of fruit and vegetables, now not much more than a pineapple-themed tourist stop with a gift shop and overpriced restaurant. Dole had an enormous influence on the development of Hawaii. Later, the company was more than a billion dollars in debt.

As Nick continued north, he came over a rise and glanced off to the left to the town of Waialua. The defunct sugar mill had become an industrial park with a soap factory, coffee roaster, surf shops, surfboard shapers, a thrift shop, and a farmers' market on Saturday mornings.

Nick turned right before Waialua, and toward Haleʻiwa, the principal town that supported the sugar mill. Now Haleʻiwa, like most of Hawaii, depends on tourist dollars to survive. The North Shore is the home of the Seven-Mile Miracle—a stretch of beach including Bonzai Pipeline, Waimea Bay, and Sunset Beach. It is an international Mecca for big-wave surfers in the winter when the surf averages wave heights of sixteen feet. The waves can reach thirty-five to fifty feet for a few weeks. It was at the break called

Outside Log Cabins, where Ken Bradshaw surfed the biggest recorded wave of 85 feet in January 1998.

Nick bypassed Hale'iwa town and continued toward Sunset Beach. It was approaching nine a.m. and traffic on Kamehameha Highway was slowing to a crawl. He flipped a switch for the electric radiator fan he had installed after overheating in traffic at the beginning of the summer. As he approached the curve at Waimea Bay and the turnoff to Waimea Falls, traffic came to a standstill. The day had heated up and the sun was pounding down on his little black car. At the end of the curve stood the white tower of the *Mission of Saints Peter and Paul*. He pulled into the parking lot where the sign read *Parking $10 Donation*, raised the top of his car, took a towel from the trunk, and stuffed it into his daypack. He left the car unlocked and the windows partly lowered, hoping the car would be left alone.

He paid for his parking and started his walk the rest of the way to Sunset Beach. On the road, drivers going in each direction stopped for him. He shot them *shaka* signs in thanks. That was a thing he liked about the North Shore; most people yielded to pedestrians.

A couple of miles later, he had passed food trucks and hundreds of tourists, many of them crowding together to watch turtles on the shore and in the shallow surf. A quarter mile later, he stopped. It was still early. Other than a woman offshore paddling an outrigger canoe, the place was deserted.

Nick looked across the white sand to the turquoise water. It was clear to the horizon with a few high clouds, and a gentle surf was churning up the sand at the water's edge. Fifty feet out, the water was a darker greenish blue where the reef started. Then the water grew lighter with splotches of sapphire blue.

Nick spread out his towel, dropped his daypack, and sat under a sea hibiscus, its yellow flowers swaying in the breeze. A hen and her five newly born chicks scratched in the leaves nearby.

Nick reached into his daypack and pulled out an apple, took a bite, broke off a piece, and tossed it to the hen, which leaped on it, quickly followed by the tiny chicks, the smallest black and white colored one the last to arrive.

Nick let out a contented sigh, feeling as though he were back in Hawaii again—the old Hawaii—before the inundation of tourists, big box stores, and intense traffic. For him, living onboard Icarus was a pleasure. Living onboard Icarus docked in Waikiki was not. There was a constant drone of humanity. Traffic, tourists, trash collection, ambulances, music coming from the bars and restaurants—it was ever present and unavoidable.

Nick was luckier than most; he could untie his home and sail it away, find another spot to drop anchor in another port or harbor on Oahu. But he was hesitant to give up his slip at the Ala Wai Boat Harbor.

Maui or Kauai? They would be much like Oahu. Both of the islands have already put in bypasses for locals to avoid tourist traffic.

Molokai? His favorite Hawaiian island, but too sleepy.

The Big Island? The volcano occasionally fouls the air and it, too had been discovered by tourists.

He had to admit he liked the conveniences of living near a city.

What about something completely different? Sail south to the Society Islands, visit his friends in Tahiti? Continue to New Zealand? Or more challenging? Sail east to Panama, take the canal to the Caribbean, and pick from the more than 700 islands there.

Nick wanted to continue to live in the tropics, and he knew tropical islands were much the same the world over.

He could continue his search for paradise, but he knew paradise was in his mind.

Nick looked out at the ocean. The water was inviting. He

stashed his backpack and towel in the bushes, ran down to the water's edge, and dove in.

Half an hour later, he got out of the water, dried off, and retrieved his belongings. He took a swig of water from his flask and noticed an opening in the foliage. He gathered his belongings and slid between branches of the sea hibiscus, coming to a clearing with a canopy of woven palm leaves. It was big enough to lay out his towel and take a nap.

The ocean waves lulled him into a deep sleep, and it was nearly two hours later when he woke. The sun had shifted and lit up the clearing. He heard children playing on the beach before he opened his eyes. Sitting up, he drank some water and retrieved the orange from his daypack. He peeled his orange and savored each bite, his body relaxed, and the stress of the city melted away.

He took the sketchbook from his backpack and for a while until the sun was directly overhead, sketched the shadow pattern of the sea hibiscus on the sand. Then he packed up his belongings, gathered the orange peels, put them in his daypack, and walked back towards Waimea Bay and his car, passing half a dozen abandoned cars in various stages of being dismantled for parts.

When Nick got back to the mission, there was an open pizza box with one slice of pizza on the trunk lid of his car. The tropical sun had already desiccated the slice. He gathered the trash and took it to a trashcan ten feet away.

SEVEN
HER NAME WAS FERAL

The next morning, Nick was sitting in the cockpit of Icarus, drinking coffee, and feeling recharged from his trip to the North Shore. *E Hula Mai* by Pandanas Club was playing on the cockpit speakers.

His mobile phone rang and he picked it up.

"What are you doing?" Willie asked.

"Just taking in the morning at the harbor."

"You sound upbeat."

"I am. I had a nice day yesterday."

Even with the traffic in both directions, getting out of Waikiki and hearing nothing but surf had a regenerative effect on his psyche. *If that's all it takes, I'll have to do it more often.*

"What are you doing up so early?" Nick asked.

"I need to bring *Caprice* over to your side. The starboard engine is still acting up."

"Do you need crew?"

"That's why I'm calling."

"Let me finish my coffee and have a bite to eat, and I'll head over."

An hour and a half later, Nick was aboard *Caprice*, Willie's forty-foot sailing catamaran. They had cast off the dock at his home on the windward side of the island and motored on one engine through Kānéohe Bay past the Hawai'i Institute of Marine Biology on Coconut Island, the blazing white sandbars already full of boats and revelers, and continued past the Marine Corps Base.

Turning right, they turned directly into the wind until they were past the eastern point of the base, then turned right again and raised the sails.

When they were past Kailua and abeam Waimānalo, Willie said, "Best beach in all the islands."

Nick took in the turquoise waters and white sand and gentle surf and had to agree. "And a great place for a full moon party. Did you see that belly dancer again?"

"No. It turned out she has a boyfriend."

"Figures."

"What about you? Weren't you seeing a woman named Savage or something like that?"

Her name was *Feral*, and Nick had met her at a client's wedding a month previously.

"I never want to be in a relationship," she said when they met.

It was an interesting opening line. Nick figured it was an exaggeration, a way to keep the distance, not let him get too close too soon. He enjoyed their first date. She suggested they rendezvous the day after the wedding in the metaphysical section of a local bookstore. She had a nice, easy smile and a vulpine way about her that appealed to him. Maybe it was her intense eye contact or the gentle touch when she made a point. To Nick, the name Feral was perfect for her. He found her mesmerizing.

Feral taught at an elementary school in Honolulu. One afternoon when she got out of class, Nick met her at the apartment she and her sister shared in Waikiki. They arrived at the same time, and he followed her up the stairs. She took off her blouse the moment she walked in the door.

"I'll be back in a moment," she said, unzipping her skirt and leaving the living room.

Nick took the time to survey the sparsely furnished apartment of mismatched reclaimed furniture. As one drove through neighborhoods in the islands, there were street corners with furniture of all kinds with *Free* signs. If you saw something you liked, it would be gone when you returned if you didn't take it then. It was the ultimate in recycling. The apartment was clean, and the furniture worked together. There was a rattan chair with a *pareo* covering the cushions and a sofa with another matching *pareo*. Woven beach mats covered the floor. Old Waikiki show posters adorned the walls, one for Don Ho and another for *The Society of Seven*. He took a seat in the chair.

He heard the shower start and run. A few minutes later, Feral came back into the living room, naked, with her hair in a towel. She plopped down onto the sofa. Her pierced left nipple had a simple gold ring hanging from it.

The scent of her shampoo—gardenia and pineapple—flowed to Nick, who sat across from her as she talked about her day—the problem children, the administration, the poor pay, and her students whom she felt would go far. It was clear to Nick she cared about her students and her job. It seemed normal, except across from him she lay nude on the sofa like in Manet's painting *Olympia*. The setting struck Nick as sexy, but not sexual.

Never wanting to be in a relationship turned out to be an accurate statement. In the three weeks she and Nick dated, she told him of her history with men. She was attracted to men like Nick. To Nick, they sounded like clean-living nice guys with good jobs from nice families.

"They all started out nice enough. Then I would find something out about them I didn't like. Then I would leave them."

"I don't know how to respond to that," Nick said.

One day, walking through Kapiolani Park after attending a hula festival, she stopped and turned to him. "You're like the rest, but even more so. You're too nice. I'm waiting for the other shoe to drop."

"Other shoe?"

"Sure. There's got to be something wrong with you. Nobody is that nice."

"I suppose if you look for something long enough, you'll find it," Nick said.

It's hard to find the right person to be with and Nick had no intention of getting involved with someone looking for problems. He wanted a long-term relationship, not something destined to fail. He cared for Feral and felt the feeling could grow. Clearly, she didn't feel the same way about him. He had no intention of waiting for her to find a fault in him, to make an excuse to not be with him.

He didn't have to.

When he got home later that night, she had sent him an email.

Hi Nick,
I had fun with you, but I can't see you anymore.
I wish you the best.
Feral

Well, that was easy.
He typed a reply.

Dear Feral,
People come into and out of our lives for many reasons.

I'm sure I'm a better person for having the privilege of spending time with you.
With Aloha,
Nick

Who says nobody is that nice? He clicked the send button.

EIGHT

WINGMAN

"That shirt again?" Willie asked.

Nick was wearing a reverse print aloha shirt of muted sunflowers.

"Hey, I live on a boat and I have a limited wardrobe. This is a great shirt." Nick ran his hands down the front, smoothing the wrinkles.

"And that scent. You're wearing your grandfather's aftershave again, aren't you?" Willie asked.

"Yes, I am. My father wore it, too, as you know. I get all sorts of compliments when I wear it," Nick said.

Willie pushed the button for the elevator. He was doing his best to get over his breakup with Helena. They were on their way to a party in a downtown luxury high-rise. Willie had long been interested in dating the hostess, who was an old family friend. He asked Nick to go with him.

"You've bounced back," Nick said.

"Getting there," Willie said.

"Wait a minute, am I your wingman?" Nick asked.

"Settle down."

"I'm your wingman, aren't I? I've always wanted to be a wing-man. Do I have any special duties?"

"Try not to embarrass me," Willie said.

The elevator car came, and they got in. Willie pushed the button for the penthouse. They rode in silence. Even in the luxury apartment building, there was a pile of shoes and slippers at the door, island style. Nick and Willie slipped out of their footwear and entered.

On the far side of the room, an elegant Polynesian woman saw them come in.

"There's Alana," Willie said.

She glided across the room toward them, not unlike a sailboat running downwind, Nick thought.

"Willie," she said, turning to Nick she added, "and you must be Nick." She kissed them on their cheeks.

"I am. Thank you for letting me join in the fun," Nick said.

"You're quite welcome. It's nice to have new people join us."

She reached forward and felt the sleeve of his shirt. "I like that shirt."

"Thank you. I was telling Willie what a great shirt this is," he said, turning to Willie.

"Okay, you win. It's a great shirt."

"And you smell great," Alana said, leaning forward for another sniff. "Is that Bay Rum? My father used to wear it."

"It *is* Bay Rum. My grandfather and my father used to wear it," Nick said, turning again to Willie.

"I give up," Willie said.

"You two are like brothers," Alana laughed. "Come, have *pupus* and meet people."

She led them into the large apartment and made introductions. It was a diverse crowd of shakers and movers, up-and-coming politicians, old island missionary family money, a few uber-wealthy, and regular folk. Nick recognized a couple of people from his consulting work around the islands. Alana slipped away to meet arriving guests.

There was a trio of string bass, guitar, and ukulele playing Hawaiian music in the corner. A bartender served drinks at a makeshift bar in another corner. Nick and Willie headed toward him; Nick ordered champagne and Willie a bottle of beer.

"Light beer, Willie?" Nick asked. "Don't you hate light beer?"

"I got used to drinking it when working on my boat. It's refreshing and doesn't have many calories."

"You should do a commercial."

Willie held the bottle up to his face and smiled for the camera.

Barefoot, Nick and Willie made their way to the buffet table. Besides the usual local fare of chow mein, manapua, ahi poke, sashimi, lomi lomi salmon, and char siu, there was also caviar and all the fixings.

Willie lifted the lid off a sterling silver chafing dish, leaned forward, and smelled the contents. "Zippy's chili," he said.

Alana came up behind them. "That's for you, Willie."

"I love Zippy's chili."

"I know you do," Alana said, continuing across the room to greet other guests.

"I'm starved," Willie said, piling a plate full of food.

Nick did the same, but with more restraint.

They walked outside past the band. The lanai was a sprawling place, with views from Diamond Head beyond Waikiki and to the airport. They sat at a table and ate.

A few minutes later, a man came to the table.

"May I join you?"

He was solidly built, but not a tall man.

"Please do." Nick and Willie stood. "I'm Nick Thomas and this is Willie Lee."

"Horatio Martín." He spoke with a South American accent.

They shook hands.

Horatio sat at the table with a plate of food. The three men ate in silence for a few moments until Horatio, turning to Nick, said, "I know you from somewhere. Don't I know you?" He had a pleasant expression on his face.

"Here we go," Willie said, putting down his fork and sitting back.

"I don't think so," Nick replied. "But I get that a lot."

Nick was hoping it was mistaken identity and not his picture in the San Francisco papers regarding the embezzlement of his company and his considerable fortune.

"I haven't seen you in Hawaii. Do you live here?" Willie asked, shoving a *manapua* into his mouth, trying to spare his friend a discussion of his past life.

"No, I don't. I have a client here who is going to leave on a trip in a couple of weeks. I came here early to visit friends and take a mini vacation."

"So, what is it you do, Horatio?" Willie asked.

"I have a private security company. We do protection for business executives and wealthy people, others with a need of safeguarding."

To Nick, Horatio exuded an indescribable level of calm.

"It must be interesting work. How do you know Alana?" Nick asked.

"I knew her father. I watched her grow up."

They went back to eating for a while. The band brought up the tempo and the music got louder. There was a burst of laughter from inside the apartment.

"So, what happens if a client gets into problems on a trip?" Willie asked.

"Depending on the situation, we would evacuate or extract the client."

"Evacuate or extract? What's the difference?" Nick asked.

Horatio put down his fork and turned to Nick.

"We evacuate someone for a medical emergency and get them to the closest doctor or hospital. Before we leave for a location, we have exit routes scouted out. Our primary goal is the client's safety."

"And an extraction?"

Horatio took a sip of wine and set it down. "In an extraction, we use our team to get the person quickly to safety. We are armed and in fast-moving vehicles to get across borders, again with exit routes defined in advance."

"So you get across a border armed and at high speed? How do you justify that?" Willie asked.

"Our primary goal is the client's safety."

Willie and Nick exchanged glances.

"Nice," Willie said, taking a bite of chili.

The three turned back to their meals.

"What's it like being a bodyguard?" Nick asked.

"It depends on the client. Some treat me like one of their inner circle or like family. I have clients who wish to have me dine at their table at social events. I have been invited to birthdays and holiday parties. Others treat me like hired help."

Willie stood up. "If you'll excuse me, I am going to get more food and talk to Alana," he said.

When Willie was gone, Horatio tried again. "I'm sure I know you from somewhere."

"Perhaps. Do you spend time in San Francisco?" Nick asked.

"No, not much. Further south in the Silicon Valley."

"Software development or aerospace?"

"I have a few clients who have software companies. I'm sure you've heard of them."

"I don't know what to tell you."

They talked more and when Horatio told Nick he enjoyed boats, Nick invited him out for a sail on Icarus.

Horatio handed Nick a card. The size was European or Asian,

slightly bigger than an American business card. It was a simple embossed linen card with his name, telephone number, email address, and logo. Nick took a closer look. The logo was a three-headed dog. "Cerberus? The hound of Hades? Quite a logo for a security company," Nick said.

"My father was a fan of classical literature. By the way, that number follows me around wherever I am in the world," Horatio said.

Meanwhile, Willie was back at the buffet table, replenishing his plate after making a tour of the room and saying hello to a few people he knew, including Jason, who stood beside him.

"Wow, this stuff is great," Jason said.

"You like that, do you?" Willie asked.

"I sure do. What is it?" He asked, swallowing a heaping spoonful.

"Caviar."

"Oh yeah, I've heard of that. It sure is good. Kind of salty. Isn't it expensive?"

Willie checked out the immense pile of eggs on Jason's plate. "I'd say you have more than $1000 worth there."

Jason looked at his plate.

"Oops."

"I'll show you how it is traditionally eaten. Watch this," Willie said.

Willie took a blini, added a dollop of crème fraîche, sprinkled on chopped egg and finely sliced onion, and topped it with caviar. "There are a few variations, but this is the gist. It's often served with ice-cold vodka or champagne." Willie popped the concoction into his mouth, chewed, and make appreciative noises. "You're not supposed to scarf it down; you're supposed to nibble at it delicately. But I have a hard time resisting."

Jason again looked at the pile of caviar on his plate. "I could see how it would go much further if you eat it that way," he said, picking up a blini and smelling it. "How did you learn to eat caviar?"

"My friend Nick taught me," Willie said, "he used to live the high life."

Off to the side, Alana watched the interaction and made her way to the buffet table. By then, a large local fellow had joined Willie and Jason. He surveyed the table of food. "There's an apple with a candle burning on the top of it," he said to Alana.

"Yes, I carved the top and put in a votive candle. I once saw an episode of Martha Stewart and I always wanted to use one for decoration on the buffet table."

The large local fellow glanced sideways at her, reached down, and took hold of the apple. He turned to Alana and said, "I hate Martha Stewart," and took a huge bite out of the apple. He set it back on the table with the candle still burning.

Alana let out a startled cry, quickly followed by a roar of laughter from her, Willie, and Jason. "This is why I invite you to my parties, Kimo. I can count on you to keep them from getting dull."

Kimo opened the lid on the chafing dish, leaned down, and took a whiff. "Zippy's chili," he said. "You've never had Zippy's chili at your parties before."

Nine

Where are you headed next?

A few days later, Horatio met Nick at Icarus. They cast off, and once out of the Ala Wai Harbor, Nick turned to the left. Then, with Horatio at the helm, Nick raised the sails and they made their way upwind toward Diamond Head.

It was clear to Nick that Horatio knew how to handle a sailboat.

"I like your boat, Nick," Horatio said, "and you keep it in excellent shape."

"I had it out of the water this time last year for maintenance and upgrades, including a new engine," Nick said.

"It shows. She's a beautiful boat."

"Thanks."

"How did you get into the security business?" Nick asked. They were both standing at the wheel. Horatio still steering.

"I learned at the knee of my father," Horatio said. "He started the business when he was in his twenties and grew it internationally. When I was old enough, he took me along on some of what he called his 'missions'."

"How old were you when you started?" Nick asked.

"I was fourteen when he first took me on protection detail."

"That must have been exciting."

"It was and still is. He retired and I run the business now."

They continued sailing until the pounding of the sea became more violent. The swells grew larger and Horatio surfed down the waves and then back up. When he reached the crest, Icarus nosed over and they shot down the wave and back up the next. Nick felt the spray of seawater on his face.

"What do you say we come about and get on a more comfortable point of sail?" Nick asked.

"Good idea. This is fun for a while, but it can get exhausting fast."

Nick moved to the jib winch, making ready to turn the boat.

"Ready to come about?" asked Horatio.

"Ready," Nick said.

"Hard a leeward."

While Nick watched him carefully, Horatio turned the bow of Icarus through the wind, expertly maneuvering through the growing swells.

They began their run downwind toward the airport.

"I've been hogging the helm," Horatio said. "I brought a nice bottle of wine. How would you like to take the wheel and I'll go below and get us a couple of glasses?"

"Sure."

They approached Honolulu Harbor while having an in-depth conversation about places they've been in the world.

"What is your favorite place to frequent on business?" Nick asked.

"I like Bangladesh. The people are great and I've made friends there."

"Where are you headed next?"

"Probably Europe, but I plan to enjoy my time here before I go," Horatio said.

"I have a consulting job that may put me in Milan next week," Nick said.

The weather was perfect and the trade winds were cooperating, so they continued past Honolulu Harbor, Honolulu International Airport, and Ewa Beach. Soon they were abeam Kalaeloa Airport, decommissioned from the Naval Air Station Barbers Point, and still home to the Coast Guard. They turned Icarus and headed back to the Ala Wai Yacht Harbor.

TEN

TO THE MANNER BORN

"I don't think I've met a person like Nick Thomas," Nigel said. Nigel and Willie were having lunch at *Buzz's Original Steak House* in Kailua on the Windward side of Oahu.

"How so?" Willie asked, taking a bite of fish.

"It's kind of hard to put into words." Nigel thought for a moment. "He's the most even-tempered man I've met. He's a bit formal—no, more like proper. But he's not stuffy and he's a lot of fun to be with. He's also very dependable. If he says he's going to do something, he will do it. He's an enigma."

"He is a modern gentleman to the manner born," Willie said.

"You knew his parents?"

"Yes, they kind of adopted me after Nick and I met at the University."

"What were they like?"

"Very proper, but very welcoming and generous. They were some of the finest people I've ever known," Willie said.

Nick Thomas was born to a moneyed San Francisco family. He was raised with old-world values in a new world. His parents held themselves to a high standard to be an example for Nick.

Those values included integrity, courtesy, showing respect—especially to women and older people, having manners, being tolerant of others, and taking responsibility for one's actions. A calmness of demeanor was also practiced in the Thomas household.

The higher standard was tempered with a caveat. "Don't judge," his father told him. "We have it better than most of the world and you don't know what others are going through."

He added a corollary, "That doesn't mean you should allow other people to take advantage of you. People may only like you for your family's money or your societal position. You need to know that."

When Nick became a teenager, his father noticed him taking an interest in girls.

One Saturday, when they were sanding and varnishing the teak on Icarus, Nick told his father. "I like Stephanie."

His father put down his brush and turned to Nick. "Stephanie? Isn't she going steady with Luke?"

"I don't think they call it going steady anymore, Father. Yes, they are an item. But she likes *me*."

"Then wait," Nick's father said.

"Wait?"

"Wait until she breaks up with Luke. Then you'll know if she really likes you or she's trying to get Luke's attention."

"Girls do that?" Nick asked.

"People do that. Besides, would you want a girl you were with to do that to you?"

"No, I guess not."

Nick's father returned to his varnishing. A moment later, he turned back to Nick. "You remember what Mark Twain said?"

"*Always do right; this will gratify some people and astonish the rest,*" Nick answered.

His upbringing made Nick confident but shy around women.

It also made him choosy about who he was with. The result confused or frustrated some women and angered others when he didn't respond to their advances.

Nick's upbringing made him an outlier nearly everywhere he went.

ELEVEN
I'll be nine days in Milan

While Suzanne continued negotiations with the Italians, Nick prepared for the trip. He made his way into town in search of an Italian language tape. He knew of a used bookstore that carried cassette tapes of every kind. Sure enough, he found one and then drove to his appointments in his Triumph. He played the Italian tape in the car's cassette stereo, an artifact from a bygone era.

"*Sono Americano,*" Nick said to the wind. *I am an American.*

"*Parlo un poco Italiano,*" said the tape. *I speak a little Italian.*

"*Parlo un poco Italiano,*" Nick repeated.

As life would have it, a fast red Italian thing pulled up beside him at a stoplight. The car contained a far-too-good-looking, tall, silver-haired man with a beautiful woman half his age. It was a cliché in motion, yet there it was.

Nick's eyes met the other driver's and then shifted to the woman. Tall, blonde, perfect white teeth, and a tiny bright orange overflowing bikini top. His eyes shifted back to those of the driver, whose nod seemed to say, "I'm doing okay for myself, eh?"

The top of the Ferrari was down, Nick's was up. He assessed

the fall Hawaiian sky and decided the silver-haired fox had the right idea. He unclasped and tossed the soft top back on his car.

Now all he needed was the girl.

"*Mólto buono!*" came a male yell from the low-slung car. The blonde beside him bounced up and down in her seat, clapping her hands and then gesturing with her thumbs up. Nick waved to the couple.

"*Le piacerebbe ballare con me?*" said the tape, the traffic light turning green. *May I have this dance?*

"*Le piacerebbe ballare con me?*" Nick echoed, putting the car into gear and accelerating through the intersection.

An hour later, Nick was sitting with Willie in ARS Café on Monserrat Avenue, just up the street from Kapi'olani Park and the Waikiki Shell amphitheater.

"So, Italy," Willie said. He took a sip of coffee and set down the cup. "With a woman," he added.

"Yes, Italy. Yes, with a woman. She's married—and has a child."

"That's too bad. How long will you be there?"

"I'll be nine days in Milan."

"How's your Italian?" Willie asked.

"I won't starve, and I can hail a taxi, find a bathroom, ask a girl to dance," Nick said.

"It's a start."

At his mother's insistence, Willie spoke Italian and Sicilian, her father's language, which Nick learned had significant differences.

"I like to talk in a mix of Italian and Sicilian. It freaks people out," Willie said.

Over the next few days, Nick and Willie spent hours together on Willie's boat. Willie taught Nick colorful and amusing phrases in Italian and Sicilian. Some would be helpful, some not, and some likely to get him into trouble.

Another week littered with tropical squalls slammed by. Once again, Nick dined with Suzanne at *Aquamarine*, and once again the oily *maître d'* directed him to Suzanne's table.

"Yesterday, Luigi sent half of our fees. He promised to pay the rest upon our arrival in Milan," Suzanne said, sipping her coffee.

"Why didn't he send the whole amount?" He asked.

"Luigi said the Italian government won't allow them to export more euros in a single day," Suzanne replied. "He said it has to do with Italy's monetary controls."

It made no sense to Nick. "That doesn't seem right. How do they get any business done? Is he going to send the balance tomorrow?"

"He didn't say."

"What do you think? Is fifty percent enough for you? We may not see another euro."

"It will be tight, but yes."

He took a sip of coffee and reflected for a moment.

"What does the rest of the cast look like?"

"Another player is Gabriella. Luigi made a slip and said Gabriella's boyfriend is funding the agency. She spends a great deal of time at the agency. I don't know what she does."

"Anyone else?"

"I've been dealing a lot with Francesca. She runs the office for Luigi and is the office manager and his assistant. She's been very helpful and responsive."

"Once we land in Milan, we should get to know Francesca better," Nick said. "It has been my experience that office managers and personal assistants often run the show."

Two days later, Nick was waiting for Suzanne at a coffee shop on Wai'alae Avenue in Kaimukī. A sign in the window read "NO BMI or ASCAP". The floors were polished concrete and there was art by local artists on the walls. The espresso bar was an immense piece of shaped wood.

"What's with the sign in the window?" Nick asked when he ordered coffee.

"An independent coffee shop like us can't afford to pay licensing fees for music and the two big publishing rights organizations, BMI and ASCAP, have been sending their enforcement agents around town."

"But you have music playing," Nick said.

"It's out-of-copyright or original music by local artists, and not registered with BMI or ASCAP, so we don't have to pay them."

"How is that working out?"

"The artists like it. Local people listen to their music, and we sell it on thumb drives. CDs are passé. If they choose to register their music, we take it off our playlist."

"How does that go over with the enforcement agents?" Nick said as a ukulele piece came on the sound system.

"The BMI and ASCAP guys don't like it at all. They keep coming in to check if we are playing other music. They usually buy a cup of coffee or something to eat, so it works out great for me."

When Suzanne arrived, they ordered coffee and sat at a table near the front window.

Suzanne took a sip. "Luigi called. He said he is interested in Emma Bedford, one of my models. He wants to put her to work in Milan." Suzanne said.

"How does that happen?" Nick asked.

"I sign her as the parent agency and I get a percentage of whatever she makes with any other agency. Usually a model signs with a specific agency in a certain locale. A model might sign with the *FIG* in Milan and *beLLeZZa* in Paris."

"So, is this a formal agreement? How do you track where your models work?"

"It's done on the honor system. People stop doing business

with them if word gets out that someone is abusing the system, model, or agency."

"I guess that could work," he reflected, taking a sip of coffee. "What else did Luigi have to say?"

"I sent your budget to him. He said it was fine and he would send the rest of the money soon."

"How soon?" Nick asked.

"He didn't say."

"I'm still fuzzy on the company structure." Nick reached for his laptop on the table between them. He opened a file he had made earlier that morning and turned the computer toward Suzanne.

"I made a chart that depicts my idea of what the structure would be like. It's rudimentary, but I had to start somewhere." The chart showed the company *swank* and Suzanne's agency at the top. Below that was the scouting company, the model camp hotel, and training center, the production company, and a new international modeling agency.

Suzanne looked at the chart. "This is how I pictured it. Do you mind if I send it to Luigi?"

"That would be a good idea. Have you learned anything about him?"

"No, but I started the process. Some of the other agencies know of him, but none of them have worked with him." She took a last sip of cold coffee. "I hope we can make this trip soon. The prêt-à-porter—the ready-to-wear—shows are coming up. It would be great to coordinate the trip with the shows," Suzanne added.

"Let's make it happen," Nick said, closing his laptop.

Twelve
You look like a Swiss banker

With their budget approved and a portion of the money sent from Luigi, Suzanne left for Milan a week later. She stopped in Los Angeles to meet with Bruce Caputo, the co-owner of a struggling modeling agency. Bruce was the one who recommended Suzanne to Luigi as a model scout. Bruce was also headed to Milan.

For as long as Nick had been in the islands, he had yet to have an extended trip requiring business attire. In Hawaii, a pressed aloha shirt, slacks, and polished shoes would put one in league with the top local executives.

Checking his wardrobe, he set out to pack clothes for the occasion. It had been years since Nick exchanged his suits and ties for aloha shirts and slacks.

He gave Willie a call.

"I have a favor to ask. I need clothes for Italy and mine are packed away in northern California."

"The new gig worked out, did it? We're still the same size. I borrowed enough of yours in the day. Come on over and take what you need."

. . .

Willie answered the door with a book in his hand, this one titled *Big Game Hunting in Alberta* by Jack Ondrack.

"Planning on going on safari in Canada, Willie?" Nick asked.

"Did you know a bull elk can grow up to 800 pounds and its antlers can get to almost five feet in length?" Willie asked.

"I did not know that."

Willie moved to the table in the foyer. "You've got to read this," he said, handing Nick a copy of *The Drifters* by James Michener.

"I have read it."

"How old were you?"

"High school?"

"You should read it again."

Later that afternoon, Nick and Willie toured Willie's closet.

"Hey, I wondered where this went," Nick said, holding up a striped tie. "I haven't seen this since our college days."

"Oh, yeah. I like that tie. I don't wear it in the islands."

"Do you mind if I borrow it back?"

"It's your tie."

Willie reached into a drawer and pulled out a jewelry box. He reached in, took out the items, and dropped them into Nick's hand. Nick looked at the cufflinks in his palm. They were in the form of boat anchors, heavy and roughly cast in sterling silver and looked as if they had been sitting in seawater and pitted with corrosion.

Nick put them on the shirt and shot his cuffs.

"Keep them. You'll use them more than I will."

"Thank you, Willie."

Nick dressed in tropical gray wool slacks, a wool blue blazer, white cotton button-down French-cuff shirt, silk socks, Italian shoes, and his long-lost tie, examined himself in the mirror.

"That ought to do it," he said.

Willie looked him up and down. "You look like a Swiss banker."

PART TWO
MILAN

Thirteen

On the plane

Nick arrived at the Newark airport two hours before the transfer to an Alitalia flight direct to Milan.

Soon he was in his seat on the plane on the ramp awaiting taxi clearance. He nodded hello to the man next to him who offered his hand, "Harrison Stafford."

"Nick Thomas. Are you going to Milan for business or pleasure?"

"I'm on my way to London. I'm stopping in Milan to meet my girlfriend and her family for the first anniversary of her aunt's death,"

"Ah," Nick said.

"It's a Jewish thing," he added.

"Ah."

Nick didn't like asking people what they did for a living. He let Harrison Stafford tell him instead.

"I'm a vice president at The Hongkong and Shanghai Banking Corporation. I'm based in New York City."

They talked and drank the Italian beer Harrison insisted on ordering for them.

"Nick Thomas," Harrison repeated, "your name is familiar.

What sort of work do you do?" he asked, pouring beer into his glass and taking a sip.

When Lance embezzled from Nick's company, the investment group was based in New York City. Nick had no desire to talk about it, so he gave Harrison an outline of his consulting in Hawaii and elsewhere.

A while later, Harrison needed to do some work before they landed in Milan. Nick took the time to read *The Drifters*, the book Willie had given him. He opened the hardback book and turned to the copywrite page. He wasn't surprised to see it was the first edition. Willie had a passion for books and his library rivaled the one Nick had inherited from his parents. Nick's books were packed away in a storage facility in a small cattle town in far northern California.

The first time Nick had read *The Drifters* he was in his teens —already well read, but still young and impressionable.

The story of *The Drifters,* set during the Vietnam era, is told through the eyes of George Fairbanks, an investment analyst for the World Mutual Bank in Switzerland. Through his travels for the bank, Fairbanks crosses paths with young people across the globe. Fairbanks befriends a diverse group of young people as they travel through Spain, Portugal, Morocco, and Mozambique, trying to make sense of a turbulent world.

A few hours later, Nick put aside his book and flipped through pages of a *USA Today* newspaper. He had picked up the paper on the way to his seat and wondered who reads it except on aircraft or when given it at a hotel. He got to the back of the paper and saw the advertisements for offshore banks. The BWI—British West Indies banks were most prominent. Harrison put his paper-work back in his attaché and slid it under the seat in front of him.

"Do you know much about offshore banks?" Nick asked. "They advertise them a lot in this newspaper."

"What do you want to know?"

"I assume they are used to launder or hide money," Nick said, speaking from experience. Offshore banks were the first stop for Nick and his investor's money when Lance embezzled it.

"There is that," Harrison replied, "but there is more to it." He signaled the flight attendant and ordered two more bottles of beer. After taking a sip, he launched into a half an hour lecture on the tax advantages, anonymity, and the liberal corporate laws of off-shore banking and corporations. He was a wealth of information and it was an incredible education.

"I wrote a paper on offshore banks when I was doing my MBA," he admitted.

"I sure asked the right person that question," Nick said.

After the lecture, they talked about the differences between living in Honolulu and Manhattan, which they both felt were as opposite as the two cultures could be.

Later, Nick got up to stretch and use the lavatory. He met a flight attendant in the aft galley. Her clothes were wrinkled, her hair a mess, and she had an exhausted look on her face.

"How are you doing tonight?" he asked.

"A bit tired, but well, thanks."

"Are you turning around and coming straight back, or do you get a day in Milan?"

"We get a day off, and then it's back to Newark."

"Tell me, how does a Kiwi get a job flying for Alitalia?"

"You're good with accents. Most Americans can't tell Aussies from Brits from Kiwis. Alitalia flights are contracted through my airline using flight and cabin crews from New Zealand."

"So how do you like the route?" he asked.

"I hate it. I can't wait until the contract is up next year."

"What don't you like about it?" He asked.

"Italy. It's very difficult doing business there."

"What makes it hard?"

"I can never get a straight answer from anyone in Italy," she said with a resigned sigh.

"So what takes you to Milan?" she asked, changing the subject.

"I'm here on business."

"Huh," she grunted. "Good luck."

Nick made his way to the lavatory to wash, shave, and brush his teeth.

Back in his seat and an hour later, Nick felt the aircraft make a gentle turn and begin its descent. Out the window, the sky had taken on a lighter shade. The day was dawning over the English Channel. From his seat, mainland Europe looked calm and inviting, as most places do after spending many hours at altitude. Soon they were on the ground and taxiing to the gate of Milan's Malpensa Airport.

FOURTEEN
ZOOM!

It was after 6:00 a.m. when Nick cleared immigration and exited the lobby of the tiny airport. He scanned the crowd of greeters. He saw no recognizable faces or people holding signs exclaiming *Nicholas Thomas*.

Harrison offered to watch Nick's bags as he exchanged money and bought a telephone card to put in the second slot in his mobile phone. As he returned, Harrison's girlfriend was arriving. She reminded Nick of a girlfriend he had in college, a brilliant and stunning Persian American. Harrison's girl Fatima was an Iraqi Jew raised in Italy and living in NYC. Harrison's eyes lit up when he saw her. Her eyes twinkled with intelligence, and her style was flawless. Her mother, beside her, revealed the source of Fatima's beauty. They thought Nick was a friend of Harrison's and the whole family welcomed him with warm embraces. He and Harrison had talked for many hours and had drunk a few bottles of Italian Beer, making Nick feel like they were old friends. They made plans to talk about potential business, and Nick took leave of his new friends to make a call. He had the foresight to get several phone numbers in Italy before leaving Honolulu. He waited until 8:00 a.m. and then dialed Francesca, Luigi's assistant at *swank*.

"*Pronto*," an irritated, sleepy voice answered.

"This is Nick Thomas. I'm traveling with Suzanne Langston and was told someone from *swank* would meet me at the airport. I've been here for two hours. No one has arrived."

"It's very early," she complained, switching to English. "Here's the address to the residence where Suzanne is staying." She rattled off the address and phone number. He read it back. Without further ado, she slammed down the phone, and Nick suspected, went back to sleep.

Nick called the *swank* residence and let the phone ring. There was no answer, and with the address in hand, he headed to the taxi stand. It was the first test of his Italian and he felt it went well. His bags were in the trunk of a Mercedes taxi and the driver had spread a map out on its trunk. Five drivers gathered around to plan the route. They were examining the address Francesca gave Nick. *Why didn't he just enter the address into the GPS?* There were many one-way streets and there was much animated discussion. He heard the word *costruzione di edifici* repeated and assumed the roads were torn up and there were detours to be considered.

The driver folded the map and turned to Nick.

"*Andiamo?*" Nick asked.

"*Andiamo*," the driver replied. Let's go.

They were off, and Nick was enjoying the view of the Italian countryside. The landscape blazed by, encouraging him to check the speedometer. Two-hundred and ten. He did a quick calculation: 130 miles per hour.

"Zoom," Nick said to the driver.

He laughed and kept his eyes on the road. "*Si, zoom. Mercedes especial,*" pleased that Nick appreciated his fast car.

Ahead, Nick saw a toll crossing for the road. The driver

shifted into the right lane and slowed down to 150 kilometers per hour. They drove through the toll plaza without reducing speed. The driver tapped a black box on the dashboard.

"*Automatique*," the driver said. As they blew into Milan, the car slowed to a crawl. The driver made a few wrong turns, looking genuinely perplexed. They turned the corner, and Nick saw Suzanne and a man walking along the street.

"*Sméttere*," Nick said to the driver, who pulled up on the sidewalk and stopped.

"Suzanne." Nick rolled down the window and called out. She spun around. Nick waved.

"We were just coming back from breakfast," she said, walking to the car. "This is Bruce. He owns an agency in L.A. He arrived last night." Nick reached out the window and shook his hand. Bruce was dressed in ragged blue jeans and a big maroon down jacket. He had brush-cut hair a la the 1950s. Suzanne was stylish as ever, wearing a leather bomber jacket with the name of a Japanese modeling agency embroidered on the back.

They stood shivering in the cool morning air.

"Why don't you get in and we can talk in the warmth?" Nick suggested. They piled in the car and told him of their adventures the previous night.

They had arrived late the night before and called Francesca from the airport.

"No one was at the airport to meet us either," Suzanne said. She told Nick how they found their way to her apartment and called from the foyer of her building. Like a twisted Italian Rapunzel, Francesca dropped the address and key for the residence down to the street from her balcony.

"When we got to the apartment, there was no heat, towels, sheets, hot water, or telephone. Winter arrived the day before; the temperature dropped twenty degrees overnight," Suzanne complained.

FIFTEEN
IT'S THE ITALIAN WAY

"Where are we going?" Nick asked. The driver waited patiently, shifting through the stations on the radio.

"I called my friend Natalie, a friend from Maui. She came to Milan to shoot fashion photography a couple of years ago. She said you and I can stay with her and her boyfriend David at their apartment," Suzanne reported.

They left their suitcases in the *swank's* marble and chrome palace and piled into Nick's taxi. They arrived at Natalie's place, another navigational feat with Milan's one-way streets.

The apartment was beside a canal with floating restaurants. It was devoid of water, as the city had drained the canals to do repairs. The restaurants sat in the mud below street level. Like many apartment buildings in Milan, the outside was unassuming. They walked in through a door cut into an enormous set of wooden double doors. Inside was a landscaped courtyard, a fountain, and another world. They made their way to Natalie's apartment on the second floor.

While Natalie and Suzanne caught up, Nick unpacked and relaxed. Bruce called Francesca on the phone and shouted at her in fluent Italian about the awful conditions of their previous night. It must have gone on for twenty minutes.

"It's the Italian way; it's the way things get done here," he said between shouts, holding his hand over the mouthpiece. Bruce had lived in Milan for two years during his modeling days and knew the ropes. The call seemed to have worked.

"Francesca will pick us up at two o'clock and take us to meet Luigi at his apartment," he said, hanging up the phone.

They had a quick caucus on how to approach Luigi. Both Suzanne and Bruce were expecting the rest of the payment for the trip upon arrival. The rest of Nick's pay was also part of the payment.

"Let's see what he does. We'll do the social thing today. Besides, no banks are open and we can't do anything until tomorrow. I suggest we enjoy the day." Nick said.

"I think you're right," Suzanne agreed.

"I need that money. I am completely broke. Sean is back in L.A. waiting for the money. We have models to pay," Bruce whined.

"Then negotiate with Luigi," Nick said, picking up his coat.

An hour later, Francesca picked them up in an ancient Fiat 500. She was pleased to meet them. Perhaps all she needed was a good night's sleep, Nick mused. They piled into her tiny black car and, driving as though she were the daughter of Mario Andretti, she took them to Luigi's second-floor apartment near the American consulate. Francesca introduced them to Luigi and then left.

Luigi was short, dark-haired, and bespectacled. His dominant characteristics were his Medici hawk nose and his eyebrows. *Ferocious* was the word Nick would use to describe the caterpillars above his eyes. Luigi was dressed in corduroy trousers, a flannel shirt, and a down jacket. The strength of his cologne made Nick's eyes water. Nick recognized it as the same cologne worn by Bruce but at a greater potency.

Luigi was pleasant enough, and he proudly gave them a tour of his apartment. It was of modern Italian style with a garden in the foyer. The floors were light oak and the walls were white. There were two-by-three-foot black and white nude photos of young Cindy Crawford, Elle Macpherson, Rachel Hunter, and a host of others. The prints were lit by theatrical floodlights hanging from the ceiling. Off-white leather sofas and wood end tables were the only furnishings. The pitch of Luigi's voice increased when he got excited talking about his apartment.

After the tour, they walked to the front of the building for a taxi waiting to take them for a brief ride to the *Ristorante Giannino dal 1899*. When they arrived, they saw polished dark wood walls and an overhang with lights in an art déco style. Inside, the dark walls and elegant furniture gave an aura of a private club.

"This family has been in the restaurant business for more than 120 years," Luigi said. "During the week, we would see celebrities, politicians, and the wealthy. They also have a restaurant in London's Mayfair district."

There was only one other table occupied in the restaurant.

"It's quiet on a Sunday afternoon," Luigi said.

The menus came and they ordered

Bruce dominated the conversation, talking non-stop in a mixture of Italian and English while Suzanne and Nick enjoyed fantastic food served on the finest china and elegant silver and crystal.

It had been thirty-eight hours since Nick had slept and he was in a sleepy haze as Bruce babbled on. Then he began negotiating for Suzanne for the structure of the new agency in Hawaii, pushing Luigi for the money promised to Suzanne and himself. He was acting like Suzanne's business manager. Nick became more alert, but kept quiet, waiting for a cue from Suzanne, who was saying nothing. By the look on her face, she was perplexed. Nick needed to know for sure, and he leaned over to Suzanne and asked, "Is this a fresh development of which I am not aware? Are you and Bruce now in business together?"

"This is the first I've heard of it," Suzanne said.

Nick sat back in his chair and listened to the nonstop blather. Bruce thought he was clever. Nick wished he would stop talking before he mucked up the process.

Bruce shut up for a minute.

Luigi turned to Nick and said to the others, "I like his style. He sits there quietly, listening. I think he has not missed a thing. I like this one."

It came to Nick that Luigi was trying to place him in the scheme of things. Nick was quiet because he was concentrating hard. He was exhausted and trying to stay awake. He had always had a problem with jet lag when he traveled east.

Nick found Luigi condescending, slick, and arrogant as if he were insecure and trying to make up for something. It made him wonder if Luigi was the decision-maker in the agency or an underling.

"I'm here to support Suzanne in her efforts," Nick responded, looking at Suzanne and not Luigi.

Nick saw Luigi for what he was, a classic misogynist. Nick deferring to a woman must have driven Luigi's Italian maleness into a testosterone frenzy. He wanted Luigi to take Suzanne seriously and was sure Luigi thought it was Nick who was making the decisions on their side.

Nick jumped into the fray. "While I appreciate Bruce's concern for Suzanne's position, Bruce and Suzanne are not business partners. Suzanne and I came to Milan to lay the groundwork for the ventures you proposed for Hawaii," he said.

After a long pause and a direct glance at Nick and pointedly, Nick felt, not at Suzanne, Luigi said, "Of course."

Bruce sat back and pouted.

Silence descended on the table.

The fatigue hit Nick in waves and, excusing himself, he went to the bathroom to splash water on his face.

The waiters came by to efficiently and quietly swap out the dinner plates for a dish of tiramisu. The quest for the perfect tiramisu was a passion of Nick's and he found tiramisu heaven at *Ristorante Giannino*. He savored every bite, as did the rest of the table. The silence was occasionally punctuated by murmurs of approval. When the last spoon was lowered, they sat back in their chairs in quiet appreciation.

The bill came and Nick caught a glance as it was delivered to Luigi. The meal for four came to 1490 euros.

He only wished he were more awake to have enjoyed it.

When the bill was paid, they rose to leave the restaurant.

"I hope I didn't overstep," Nick whispered to Suzanne on the way out.

"Not at all."

Sixteen

By the time they returned to Luigi's apartment, Nick had a second wind. Then again, it could have been the company. Joining them were Valentina Moretti whom Luigi mentioned during lunch was involved with *swank*, and Alessandra and Corrine, two models from Brazil. Valentina was once an agent with Ford Models in São Paulo. Alessandra and Corrine were models in town for the shows. Nick sat next to Alessandra, whom he found to be intelligent and articulate. Once scarred from a motorcycle accident, she had had extensive cosmetic surgery and was back in the modeling business. Nick took a good look at her. He could see no evidence of any damage.

"You must enjoy modeling to get back into it after your accident," he said

"It's very lucrative, and my agency has been supportive."

"Do you enjoy it?" Nick asked.

"Much of the time I do. Although lately, models have sabotaged other models before runway shows by destroying or hiding clothes and shoes."

"That's a terrible idea. I can't imagine they would ever work again if the designer learned who they were," Nick said.

"Yes, their careers would be over."

Catfights on the catwalks, Nick thought.

They stopped at the *swank* residence where Suzanne collected her bags and Nick hung back to talk to the taxi driver, leaving Bruce behind. When Suzanne got back in the taxi and the door shut, she gave out an enormous sigh.

"What was that about with Bruce?" Nick asked.

"I have no idea," Suzanne said.

"That guy Bruce is dangerous. I can't recommend you do any work with him. He is quickly becoming a liability."

"I have no intention of working with him," Suzanne said.

Back at the apartment, Suzanne and Nick moved into the loft. It was up a narrow steel staircase with creaky hardwood treads. At the top, the staircase divided the open-air room with beds on each side. Natalie used the room for her children who visited from Maui. Nick got the son's side featuring the twin bed with dinosaur sheets. Suzanne got the daughter's side, another twin bed with Barbie sheets. The room had skylights, which opened and closed with the temperature. It was a tall room with lots of natural light.

Nick gave Suzanne privacy so she could dress for dinner with Luigi and the backer of *swank*. In the salon downstairs, Nick got to know Natalie and David. Natalie was a model turned photographer and had a brilliant eye for composition. Her photos adorned the walls of her apartment. They were high contrast black and whites, most of them nudes of both sexes. David was a model and was in many of the photographs with different female models, and Natalie.

After a half-hour visit, Nick headed back to the loft to get his laptop.

"Are you decent?" Nick called to Suzanne from mid-span on the stairs.

"Decent enough," Suzanne replied, and Nick continued his climb.

She was straddling a chair, arms across the backrest, applying mascara. She wore a black brassière and tight black panties. Her long legs completed the picture. She met his eyes in the mirror.

Nick took a strong breath and shook his head. *Settle down, Nick. She's a client, and she's married.*

Her expression gave him the indication she knew exactly what he was thinking. Her face held a slight smile.

Nick gathered his laptop and took it downstairs. Later, when Suzanne joined them, Nick said, "I'm happy to accompany you if you wish."

Suzanne took one look at Nick and said, "Get some rest so we can tackle this tomorrow. Tonight should be a social function."

Natalie, David, and Nick talked a while longer and headed to dinner at a pizzeria and karaoke place down the street. In Hawaii, karaoke is popular. Seeing it in Italy with Italian subtitles was too much for Nick's jet-lagged brain. They ate pizza and drank *Chiaretto*, a dry rosé, slightly carbonated, strong, and harsh.

They walked home around eleven thirty. Still awake and his body confused by the time change, Nick picked up his book.

Suzanne got home around 1:30. Nick heard her try to quietly climb the stairs, but the wood treads squeaked and metal railings creaked.

"How was dinner?" Nick asked.

"Dinner was fine. I'm beat. Tomorrow I'll tell you how it went."

"Okay. *Buena note.*" Nick said, closing the book and setting it on the nightstand. He was asleep in minutes.

Seventeen
Julian Hoffstetter

Across the border in Zürich, a banker named Julian Hoffstetter was enjoying his morning cup of coffee on the sunny patio outside his office. The weather had cooled and he could smell the smoke from his neighbor's fireplace.

The women in Hoffstetter's life were becoming troublesome. Gabriella, his Italian girlfriend, was causing the most fuss. She was determined to get into the modeling industry. Not as a model, although Julian Hoffstetter felt she was attractive enough for it, but in management. After studying the business, she concluded that was where the excitement was, and to the relief of Hoffstetter, she headed to Milan to explore her opportunities.

After Gabriella presented Hoffstetter with her plan for the modeling agency, he gave her his blessing to go ahead. He only had two requirements. The first was his name to be kept out of the business entirely. The banking world in Zürich was a conservative one. He would set up a holding company and a go-between in Switzerland for her to deal with, insulating him from the business. The second requirement was she find an existing agency and take it over, jumpstarting her into the business.

On her first trip to Europe, Gabriella met Luigi Donato in the waiting room of *beLLeZZa* Milano, a top agency in Milan. While they waited for their meetings, they talked. Their plans were similar and Luigi, noticing Gabriella's designer fashions and expensive jewelry, saw her as a source of funds. He convinced her he was the one she needed to set up and run an agency in Milan.

Eighteen

What is your name?

Nick opened his eyes to the bright blue sky visible through the skylights above his bed. He winced at the brightness. *Who puts skylights above beds?*

He picked up his journal from the bedside table and recorded the previous day's events. His fountain pen was empty and made scratchy noises on the paper. He sleepily retrieved an ink cartridge from his suitcase, climbed back into bed, wrote for ten minutes, and then got on with the day.

Wearing old black karate pants and a *Kenwood Cup Yacht Race* t-shirt, Nick made his way barefoot down the creaky stairs to the kitchen and poked his head out the window to look at the street below. It was quiet and the sun was shining in and bouncing off the high white walls of the apartment. He made espresso, filling the kitchen and the rest of the apartment with the aroma of strong coffee. A voice behind him said, "That smells wonderful."

He turned to see Suzanne standing in the kitchen doorway. She was wearing a brightly colored negligée over a matching night-gown. It was an odd picture, she with her sleepy face and bare feet. Suzanne appeared natural as if the two of them had been doing this for years: him getting up early and making coffee on a

Monday morning and she coming to join him when the aroma encouraged her to wake. Nick had the sudden and curious feeling he and this woman had been knocking around the planet together for a millennium or two.

"Make yourself comfortable," Nick said, pouring espresso into a cup. "Milk?"

"Please." He got milk from the refrigerator and added it to her cup, then searched the cupboard for something to go with the coffee. He found a tin of biscuits and took a nibble, then put a few on a plate and handed the biscuits and coffee to Suzanne. She padded to the table and sat; Nick poured his cup and joined her.

They looked across at each other. She took a sip.

"Great coffee and so are these biscuits," she said, taking a bite.

"How was dinner?"

"It was fine. We went to a nice restaurant and then to a nightclub. We didn't talk a word of business. One guy who joined us was from an investment group in Switzerland. The food was good, but the company was kind of boring. I don't have much to report. It was a night of small talk."

Nick took a sip. "We should define our strategy for the week. Why don't we rerun the numbers for the first scouting trip and add the numbers for Paris and London? Then we can give Luigi an update."

For the next hour, they worked on the budget and schedule for the first round of scouting trips Suzanne would make. They separated the scouting trips to Sweden and Greece so Bruce could do them on a separate schedule.

Nick grimaced when he plugged his laptop into the Italian power grid. There were no sparks or other indications of pain from the computer: he went to work on the budget for a couple of hours.

After a quick bath, he dressed for business, going with his most formal attire: gray wool slacks, French cuff white shirt, understated silk tie, a wool blue blazer, topped off with a Swiss watch, and Swiss shoes and belt. He attached his anchor cufflinks and made his way down the stairs. He found Suzanne in a stylish flowered dress, looking the part of a model agency owner.

"You look elegant. I'm impressed you had those clothes in Hawaii."

"Thanks. You look posh yourself." He would have to remember to thank Willie again.

Suzanne and Nick continued their discussions as they waited for their driver to call from the street. The phone rang, and they walked down to the cut-out wood door. There, standing beside an Alfa Romeo sedan, was their driver.

"My name is Massimo," he said, offering his hand to them. They introduced themselves and he opened the front and rear doors. Suzanne climbed in the front, Nick in the back.

Massimo was from Turino, a city to the southwest. Nick again watched Italy blast by down the narrow streets of Milan. At one point the street became tighter and Nick saw Massimo push a button and the right side rear-view mirror folded toward the window, giving the car an extra couple of centimeters clearance, enabling him to zoom through narrow openings without reducing speed. From the right rear seat, it looked as if they would take the paint off the parked cars.

At first sight, Milan gave Nick the impression of a city where wealth had been centered for millennia. The second most populous city in Italy after Rome, Milan had been ruled by the Celts, Romans, Goths, Lombards, Spaniards, and Austrians. When the Austrians left Milan, it became part of the Kingdom of Italy and Milan evolved into the industrial, commercial, and financial capital of the country. It shares the title of the capital of fashion with Paris.

Nick took in Milan as it sped by. With the graffiti on the once beautiful buildings and the homeless on the streets, the city appeared ripe for another rebellion of the commoners against the nobility, as happened during some of the changeovers of power in Milan's history.

Fifteen minutes later, Massimo deposited them at the front of the *swank* offices and they took the elevator to the third floor. The office was populated with a couple of women bookers who arrange the work for models and a male administrative assistant dressed in all-black denim with a black leather bandolier and wide black leather belt with metal studs. The bookers were stationed at a huge, oval black table in the main room. They sat reading fashion magazines when not going outside to smoke cigarettes. Going outside didn't help; the office reeked of cigarette smoke and Luigi and Bruce's cologne.

Francesca sat in an office off to the side. Beyond that was a hallway leading to other offices. Luigi's office was the first past the bookers' bullpen.

The monochromatic office had framed black and white photos of models on the walls. Nick perused the models' portfolios and their cards on a table while Suzanne walked from framed print to framed print, shaking her head.

"These are my models. I represent them and have exclusive contracts with them. Why does Luigi have framed photos of them on the walls of his agency? There's Emma Bedford, my newest model. Where did he get that photograph?" Suzanne asked.

"You should ask him," Nick said.

"I intend to."

Francesca led Nick and Suzanne to Luigi in his office. They made pleasantries and chitchat about the previous day.

"Luigi, I see you have photos of many of my top models on the walls of the lobby," Suzanne said.

"Yes. I'm sure we will come to an arrangement soon," Luigi said.

"It seems a bit premature," Nick said.

Luigi turned to Nick. "What is your name?"

Nick turned to him with a deadpan expression. He reached into his pocket and withdrew a business card and handed it to him.

It was an interesting opening gambit, and Nick was sure, the beginning of a power struggle between them.

A woman appearing in the doorway interrupted them.

Luigi gestured to the woman. "This is Gabriella, a backer of the agency."

Nick stood, smiled at her, and shook her hand.

"*Ciao*, I'm Nicholas Thomas," Nick said.

"*Ciao*, Nicholas. Hello, Suzanne. Nice to see you again."

Gabriella took a seat next to Nick.

Luigi looked at his watch. "I need to make a phone call," he said, standing and heading towards the door.

Suzanne was next, standing. "I think I'll take the time to call some agencies. I'll catch up with you before lunch, Nick. Nice to see you again, Gabriella."

When they were alone, Nick turned to Gabriella. "I thought they would never leave."

"I thought I chased everyone off when I came in," Gabriella countered.

"Perhaps my cologne clashed with Luigi's," Nick said.

Gabriella let out a laugh. It was high-pitched and ended in a snort.

"Sorry," she said, covering her mouth. She giggled and snorted again.

Nick couldn't help but laugh. Gabriella leaned forward and took a sniff of his shoulder. "Your cologne is nice," followed by yet another giggle and snort.

Maybe it was the jet leg, but her laughter was infectious. Soon, they were laughing and snorting away. Nick pulled out his mobile phone and recorded it.

"I shouldn't have done that. I'll delete it," he said.

"No, no. It's quite all right. I've lived with it all my life. My brothers still tease me. It's a part of who I am."

"That is a healthy attitude. Good for you," Nick said. He took her in. She was polished and expensively dressed, wearing a sapphire and diamond suite of jewelry—earrings, necklace, bracelet, and matching ring.

Nick and Gabriella chatted while Luigi and Suzanne were making their calls. Nick learned she was twenty-four, from Romania, had married young, divorced, and got out of Romania. She heard Switzerland was filled with millionaires and billionaires. She saved her money and bought a train ticket to Zürich, leaving Romania with a suitcase of her best clothes and little money.

"I met a man at a café the day I arrived in Switzerland. He invited me to dinner that night. We have been together ever since."

Nick found her engaging and sophisticated, in a nouveau riche Romanian-peasant sort of way. He shuddered at the thought, realizing he had acquired some snobbery growing up in the upper echelons of San Francisco society.

"So how did you come to oversee the investment of *swank*?" Nick asked.

"Er, um. My boyfriend helped me."

Suzanne was the first to return to the office, followed a few minutes later by Luigi, who announced, "It's time for lunch. *Andiamo*."

When they arrived at the front of the agency, Massimo was waiting for them.

"I don't know where we are going," Nick said.

"Luigi texted me. *Ristorante Corte Sant'Andrea*. The others will meet us there," Massimo said.

When they arrived, the *maître d'* greeted them and showed them to their table.

After they sat, Suzanne turned to Nick. "I'd like to get a better idea of where we stand."

"Maybe we can have a genuine conversation with Luigi—with him and Gabriella," Nick said. "Maybe not," he added, seeing Bruce and Valentina precede Luigi and Gabriella into the restaurant.

Gabriella moved to sit next to Nick and Suzanne, obviously intending to continue her conversation with Nick.

Perhaps it was because Gabriella was present, but Bruce didn't dominate the conversation with his pleading for cash.

The conversations at lunch were conducted in English, French, Italian, and Brazilian Portuguese, and lasted until 3:00 p.m. with no business conducted.

Nick had the sea bass ravioli.

Suzanne and Nick met with Luigi in the *swank* conference room upon their return.

"I have forgotten your name," Luigi said.

Nick resisted rolling his eyes and didn't act insulted. He pulled another business card from his pocket and handed it to him.

"We would like to discuss the plan for the company in Hawaii," Suzanne said.

"Here is the business plan," Luigi said, sliding copies across the table to each of them.

Nick picked up his copy and flipped through it. There was nothing to it, a few pages, no numbers, and, of course, in Italian. But there was a corporate organization chart and that was clear enough. The chart had an investment corporation at the top, a corporation with "B.W.I." in parentheses below, then Agencies A, B, C, D, and E below that. No detail, only letters.

The "B.W.I." caught Nick's attention.

"British West Indies? Is this an offshore corporation?" he asked, pointing to the first box on the chart.

Surprise crossed Luigi's face, and then his brow furrowed.

"Yes," he said simply.

"Why use an offshore corporation?" Suzanne asked.

"Offshore corporations are typically not subject to the taxation of their home jurisdiction. Also, regulations for offshore corporations are much less stringent than in most developed countries." *That talk on the plane with Harrison Stafford came in handy.* He would tell her the money laundering aspects later.

Nick turned to Luigi. "Where in the British West Indies?"

"The Cayman Islands."

Nick turned back to Suzanne. "And the Caymans have some of the most strict privacy laws for corporations. There is virtually no public information available on the ownership or board members. "

Nick turned back to Luigi, who sat with his arms crossed in front of him and a furrowed brow.

"Why are you here?" he asked.

"I'm here to assist Suzanne since she will be busy scouting," Nick replied.

"Are you a financial expert?" he asked.

"No."

"Then you are a lawyer."

"No, I have people to do that for me. I oversee entire deals, not just the pieces. If I need a lawyer, I bring one in. If I need financial accounting, I find it." It sounded more organized than it was. In actuality, Nick had a group of friends who passed work back and forth. Willie, being a financial wizard, was one of them. If it appeared arrogant, it was intentional. Nick was jockeying for position.

Luigi said nothing and stared at Nick from across the table.

Luigi reached into a folder and pulled out the chart Nick had designed in Hawaii.

"This is what we are to do," he said, handing the diagram to Nick, who scanned it and slid it back to him.

"Yes, that should do," Nick told him flatly.

It became the basis for the rest of the discussions that evening. Had Luigi done no preparation? Where did he think the chart came from? There were email headers from Hawaii and Milan on it. Perhaps he thought it had been produced in Milan and sent to Suzanne in Hawaii.

Luigi was competitive, that was obvious. He needed to be the big dog, the big man on campus. Nick let him. It was the wrong approach on Luigi's part. Nick sat back in amusement and watched Luigi strut around his office.

"Luigi, I want the remainder of the funds from you, the amount we agreed upon before I left for Hawaii," Suzanne said.

"I need to go to Switzerland for the money," Luigi said, dismissing the subject with a wave of his hand.

Italy has had a new government on average every thirteen months since 1945. Taxes are high and people leave their money across the border in Switzerland for financial security.

It is a short ride past the southern tip of beautiful Lake Como into the next country, a few hours for a round trip in one of those fast Mercedes taxis. But crossing the border for money was no longer necessary, as electronic transfers were legal. But Luigi enjoyed the fast drive, and it gave him time to plot his next move.

"Time is short," Suzanne continued. "I need to go to Paris next week for the shows, and Nick may head to Greece to see his family."

"You have family in Greece?" Luigi asked, turning to Nick.

"Yes. But they travel a great deal and will only be there until Saturday."

"What does your family do?"

"They're in shipping."

Luigi pushed back his chair, crossed his arms, and stared at him. Nick looked at Suzanne, who registered Luigi's reaction.

"I've run numbers on the cost of Suzanne's scouting trips," Nick told him. He turned his laptop so Luigi could see the spreadsheet. His mobile phone beeped. Or rather, it produced a lilting laugh, followed by a snort.

"What was that?" Luigi asked.

"That was Gabriella."

"Gabriella?"

"Gabriella. I recorded her voice this morning. Now my phone has her laugh whenever I receive a text message."

Once again, Luigi pushed his chair back, crossed his arms, and stared at Nick.

They got through the discussion of Suzanne's scouting budget. But before the discussion ended, Nick asked, "Luigi, where do you see *swank* in five years?" It was one of those obnoxious questions that are good to ask an entrepreneur. The answer is a gauge of the person's drive, passion, and, most importantly, realism.

"Within five years, we will be the largest modeling agency in Europe. In ten years *swank* will be the number one company in the world in modeling, film, and music," Luigi answered with zeal and pride.

"So you are not going to constrain your work to Italy and Europe? You are going to America and Asia to dominate those markets?" Nick asked.

"Within ten years, we will be the biggest in the world for all of those industries," he said, pounding his fist on the table and his voice raising in pitch, his eyebrows flapping as if they would soon depart his face.

Nick questioned him on the details for a few minutes. How did he plan to get there? What inroads had he made? What alliances had he formed? Like his business plan, it was ill-defined. He had plans, but they were unfocused.

Nick tried not to look disappointed. *Great, another egotistical visionary entrepreneur. These guys are the same the world over, but this one was far out of his league and swank is the perfect name for his agency.*

Nick couldn't imagine Luigi being taken seriously in Milan. In one of the most formal cities in Italy, the guy dresses like a lumberjack. If he were really powerful, he wouldn't be talking to him and Suzanne; he'd have an underling do it. He'd be wining-and-dining heads of industry. No, there was something else going on here. He has funding from a source to pay for this office in a prime location. Perhaps the agency is a plaything for Gabriella's boyfriend.

Maybe time would tell.

Nick tried his best to not show disappointment, disbelief, or outright hilarity.

"Well, Luigi, if that is what you are planning to do, I'm sure you will be successful," he said, trying his best not to sound sarcastic.

Suzanne gave Nick an incredulous look.

Luigi beamed at the comment.

With Nick's closing line, Luigi stood, indicating the meeting was over.

"I have arranged with *Ristorante Corte Sant'Andrea*. You may go there for all of your meals if you wish and put them on my account," Luigi said.

Back in the car on the way to the apartment, Nick and Suzanne rode in silence, both lost in thought.

"You weren't serious, I hope. About Luigi being a world power?" Suzanne said, breaking the silence.

"Of course not."

They rode in silence again until Suzanne said, "We should plan a cocktail party."

"A cocktail party?"

"Yes. I'll invite agency owners and bookers, all the shakers and movers."

"We have it at the apartment?" Nick asked.

"I'm sure Natalie will go along. It will be great for her work as a photographer to network with the people I'll invite. I'm sure it will help David with his modeling, too."

"Okay then," Nick said.

"By the way, you may want to air out your suit. After spending so much time in the office, you smell like Luigi and Bruce. And cigarettes."

"We both do," Nick said.

NINETEEN
IS THIS NORMAL?

The next morning, Nick reached for his pen and journal and reviewed the previous day. He found if he did it in the evening, he would have trouble getting to sleep.

The workday at *swank* started after 10:00 a.m., and when Nick and Suzanne arrived at the offices of the agency, the bookers were straggling in. Luigi was nowhere in sight.

"Is this normal?" Nick asked.

"Not during the week of the shows. No, it isn't normal," Suzanne said.

They headed to an empty office and opened their laptops.

"I'm not used to being so unproductive," Nick said.

"Me, either."

A few minutes later, Nick saw Francesca come in. She dropped her purse at her desk and made espresso at the coffee station. She stopped at the office door,

"Luigi has gone to Switzerland for money," she said, and then left.

"I guess we have a day to ourselves," Suzanne said. "Let's talk to the other agency owners. I might as well get business done for myself while Luigi is chasing cash."

"I'll call Massimo and have him bring the car," Nick said.

TWENTY
Luigi Donati

If one went back far enough in the lineage of Luigi Donati, one would indeed find the source of his Medici hawk nose. The Donati was a Tuscan family, as was the House of Medici before the Medici expanded their way north to Florence. There, in the 15th century, the family founded the Banco dei Medici, which at the time was the most powerful bank in Europe. The Medici family dynasty included four popes, solidifying their political power in Europe.

Luigi was proud of his Medici nose. He didn't know it came from a 400-year-old liaison of a Medici banker and a local barmaid. The bastard child was sent to a convent and he and his nose disappeared into the ether of history.

Where the ferocious eyebrows came from was anyone's guess.

Luigi Donati was a troublesome child with a hot temper. His parents, prominent attorneys in Rome, sent him to boarding school when he was five years old. It was young by Italian standards, but the school took children as young as two. Luigi liked nothing about the school and would sneak out and flag down a passing vehicle for a ride. When asked why he wasn't in school, he would make up an elaborate and convincing story. The headmaster would have to send someone to retrieve him. Once he caught a ride on a truck and made it nearly 300 kilometers to the North.

When he attended classes, Luigi argued with the teachers, staff, and students. He cheated at games and on his coursework. He was so clever at hiding notes, that the teacher took to sitting at the desk next to him when he took his exams.

By the time Luigi was eight, he was expelled and sent to live with his grandparents in the hilltop village of *Poggio Santa Cecilia* in the Siena district of Tuscany. His parents, absorbed in their law practice in Rome, had given up on the child.

The village, built on the ruins of a medieval castle dating back to the year 1200 was nearly deserted when Luigi arrived. Most of the residents had moved to larger villages and nearby towns for work.

Luigi saw the place as a prison. In the afternoons, he would stand at the gate and gaze longingly at the towns down the hill.

Like Luigi's father, his grandfather, Giuseppe Donati was an attorney. He and Luigi's grandmother, Maria, had left Rome for the quiet life in the country where he focused his legal work on real estate and the occasional family trust. When Luigi arrived at *Poggio Santa Cecilia*, Giuseppe Donati took it upon himself to educate the boy. Unlike Luigi's parents and teachers, Luigi's grandfather accepted no quarter from his grandson. Perhaps it was his height, baritone voice, and strength of character honed by years as a top litigation attorney in Rome. Luigi's argumentative personality didn't stand a chance against Giuseppe Donati.

It wasn't long before Luigi tried to escape down the 1,300-foot hill to get as far away as possible from his grandparents. He soon learned his grandfather had put out the word in the surrounding countryside there would be severe legal problems for anyone offering a ride to his grandson.

Luigi would be stuck on a hilltop, homeschooled by his grandfather, whom he quickly learned he could not manipulate. He received a first-class education. Luigi and his grandfather would stroll the grounds of the village, Luigi reciting his recent lessons and the Latin names of any plant they came across. By the time Luigi graduated from homeschool, he could read and write in English, French, and German to go along with his Italian.

In addition to the core studies of math, science, reading, writing, geography, and social studies, Giuseppe Donati taught him what he knew best, the law. He used his former cases as examples. It was the one subject Luigi took to with a passion. His grandfather had to insist he finish his other studies before getting back to it. The grandfather would often find Luigi late at night reading dusty old law books in the villa library. The next morning at breakfast, they would discuss a case or a ruling

What really caught Luigi's attention were the cases of organized crime. He studied those without his grandfather's knowledge. He examined how and why cases were won and lost and compiled a list of defendants and the organizations they worked for. Luigi was fascinated by all aspects of their business whether it be money laundering, counterfeiting, prostitution, the selling of drugs or arms, extortion, or blackmail.

One thing bothered Luigi's grandfather. Luigi had no regard for other people and lacked a conscience.

Once, when Luigi and his grandparents were in the nearby village buying groceries, they saw a man hit a pothole in the road and fall off his bicycle. While the grandparents hurried to help, Luigi stood on the street corner and laughed hysterically, imitating the way the man swerved and then crashed.

When the teaching turned to the law and ethics and doing the right thing for the sake of it, Luigi wanted to know, "What's in it for me?"

When Luigi was ready to leave the hilltop hamlet for university, the place was nearly abandoned. The lack of employment coupled with a severe drainage issue finished *Poggio Santa Cecilia*. His grandparents were the last inhabitants. A few years later, they moved back to Rome, where they had kept an apartment.

In their will, Luigi's grandparents left their villa in *Poggio Santa Cecilia* to Luigi. He never wanted to go back to the deserted village. Luigi later exchanged the property to pay off a 1000 euro debt. Six years later, he saw an advertisement for the sale of the entire village. The Italian countryside was going through a real estate boom. The asking price was 44 million euros.

With his grandfather's training for academic achievement and a leg up in legal studies, Luigi breezed through the University of Milan with a Master of Laws degree and an eighteen-month legal apprenticeship at a law firm.

Once out of school, he was offered positions at the most prestigious firms in Italy, and he went to work at the one offering the most money.

As with any entry-level lawyer, Luigi started on the bottom rung. He had been studying law with his grandfather since he was ten years old, and at twenty-five, he knew more about the law than many of his seasoned colleagues.

Luigi lived lightly in a compact, inexpensive apartment and banked his cash. By the time he was thirty, he had the seniority to move up in the company. He had the reputation of a competent attorney who was difficult to work with.

Years later when Luigi was passed over for promotion, he explored other opportunities. He had kept his list of members of organized crime organizations and cautiously reached out. From his years of studying cases, he was able to offer his expertise on how to avoid getting caught and prosecuted.

Luigi was given a trial run, and his success led to legal consulting paid in cash. Over time, he met a wide range of members of the organization and expanded his involvement.

One October, during the fashion shows in Milan, Luigi was struck by the money and power descending upon the city. Money and power were things he had always craved.

The week after the shows, Luigi talked his way into a meeting at *beLLeZZa,* where he met Gabriella.

Twenty-One

So this is what a real agency is like

The *Piazza del Duomo* is the geographical and historical center of Milan and the home of the Milan Cathedral. The rest of Milan spreads out from there, with a ring road surrounding the center, which approximately follows the *Cerchia dei Navigli,* a floodable moat—a ring of walls dating back to the year 1156, enclosing and protecting the medieval center of Milan.

So far, Nick and Suzanne had not strayed out of the ring road of Milan. That day was no exception, as Massimo drove them to their first stop.

As they drove through Milan, Nick took in the people. Those who had the resources were generally well turned out and elegantly attired.

Noticing Nick, Massimo said, "People in this part of town put on Versace suits to get the newspaper."

Nick had never seen more beautiful women in one spot.

"The models are arriving for the shows," Massimo said. "Milan will be filled with the most beautiful people in the world," he added.

Perhaps, Nick thought, but a non-anorectic Polynesian

woman with waist-length hair could give this scene in Milan a moment's pause.

What Nick noticed straight away was the way the women in Milan delivered eye contact. It was unnerving at first, but to him, the people were genuinely friendly in a Hawaiian aloha sort of way. He had heard the stories of the dark side of Italy and had women friends who had been accosted by Italian men, and friends overcharged by taxis and abused by gypsies. He had heard the bad side of every country he visited. But he tried to recognize the humanity in everyone he met. If you treat a taxi driver as a taxi driver and not as a fellow human, you're asking for trouble. It comes through in any culture. It was another value his parents had instilled in him.

The first agency they visited was *beLLeZZa*, in the Porta Monforte district.

"So this is what a real agency is like," Nick said when they entered the lobby.

Phones were ringing, people were rushing in and out. It was controlled chaos. The energy was intense because of the prêt-à-porter shows. Nick couldn't help but think about the *swank* office, with the bookers sitting around reading magazines and stepping out to smoke.

Four modeling agencies later, it was late in the afternoon and their last call was *FIG*—Fashion International Group, a top agency near the *Fiera*, the location for the upcoming fashion shows.

On the wall of the lobby of the agency was the logo—a fig.

The models at the agency were as beautiful as one would expect.

"I want to talk to a couple of scouts I've worked with. I'll be a little while," Suzanne said.

"I'll be fine here in the lobby," Nick said.

Suzanne left and Nick found a comfortable chair. He flipped through a stack of magazines on a nearby table and picked out the Italian edition of Architectural Digest. He opened the magazine and saw where Luigi got the inspiration for the design of his apartment. His was a carbon copy of one featured in the pages. Nick's reading was interrupted by a tall, brunette woman opening the door. She had a retro 1960s thing happening, her brown hair up and back.

"*Ciao*," she said, dropping into the seat beside him.

"*Buongiorno*," Nick said.

"Oh, thank God, you're American."

"I am."

"Cash," she said, reaching out her hand to shake.

Nick extended his hand, a quizzical look on his face. "Nick?"

"It's the name I go by when modeling. *Cash*."

"That's the reason to be in this business," Nick said.

"Hah. You've got that right."

"How has your day been?" Nick asked.

"So far, I've been to fourteen castings today. I only have two more to go!"

To Nick, she was as fresh as if she had just started the day.

Twenty-Two
Scouting for a Princess

That evening, Suzanne and Nick found themselves at dinner at *Ristorante Corte Santandrea* with Valentina and Bruce.

The *maître d'* came by and informed them, "Senor Donati has informed us he has taken care of your account for the next week." He dropped off two bottles of water, one carbonated, one still.

"*Grazie*," Nick replied.

They sat back and perused the menu.

"Luigi promised me money. I need to get it back to my boyfriend in LA. He's running the agency while I'm gone," Bruce said.

"Luigi promised me money, too," Suzanne said.

"And me," Valentina said.

"But I need it. Our agency is hurting," Bruce whined.

"At least he remembers your names," Nick said. "I'm going to run out of business cards if he keeps asking me."

"Luigi knows who you are," Valentina said, taking a sip of wine.

"Yes, that's what I thought," Nick said. "Interesting tactic."

Nick wondered if they would ever see the rest of the money Luigi promised. Nick considered Luigi living high in his beautiful apartment. He seemed the type of guy who would use you as far as he could and then never pay you. With that in mind, he made up for it straight away. He gestured to the *maître d'*.

"Do you have Bollinger Champagne on your wine list?" Nick asked him.

"*Mi dispiace, signore.* We do not have Bollinger, but we do have Dom Pérignon."

"That will be fine, thank you," Nick said.

The waiter took their orders, and when he left, Nick said to no one in particular, "To me, Luigi fits the profile of a gambler."

"A friend here told me Luigi had been up tens of millions and now he is back down to zero. He is behind in rent and has a host of other bills," Valentina said.

Suzanne caught Nick's eye and raised an eyebrow.

There was silence around the table as it sunk in.

Valentina was the first to break the silence. "The Emir was staying at Luigi's. He left last Friday."

"The Emir?" Suzanne asked.

"A prince of one of the Middle Eastern monarchies," Valentina replied.

"A Middle Eastern prince has been staying with Luigi?" Nick asked.

"He fancies himself the Prince Rainer of the Middle East. According to Luigi, he's obsessed with the House of Grimaldi."

"Well, who isn't?" Bruce chimed in.

Nick lifted his hand to be counted as one who wasn't obsessed with the House of Grimaldi.

"Luigi was introducing him to a lot of models," Valentina said.

"That's more than creepy," Nick said, turning to Suzanne.

"Funny, they all had a Grace Kelly look to them," Valentina said.

"Wow," Nick said. He didn't like where the conversation was heading.

"When the Emir learned you didn't bring Emma along with you...." Valentina said.

"Excuse me?" Suzanne asked.

"When the Emir learned you didn't bring Emma along with you, he went home," Valentina finished.

It was like she had dropped a bomb in the middle of the table.

Suzanne and Nick exchanged troubled glances.

"Emma looks a lot like Grace Kelly. She could play her convincingly in a movie of her life," Valentina said.

The waiter arrived with the champagne, opened it, and filled the glasses at the table. He left the bucket in a stand beside him and departed.

They stared at their glasses. Finally, Nick lifted his glass and took a sip. He thought what his friend Francois in Tahiti said of Dom Pérignon was right; it tastes like dust. But it was crisp, dry, and had tight bubbles.

Nick set his glass down on the table. "This may make a great movie someday," Nick said.

"You could call it *Scouting for a Princess*," Valentina offered.

The discussion of the Emir and his search for a princess was cut short when waiters arrived with their dinners. While they ate, Bruce and Valentina talked of putting together a supermodel contest with preliminary pageants in Brazil and Los Angeles, with the final pageant contest in Hawaii. There was a great deal of money to be made producing the contest independently of *swank* and Luigi. It was odd to Nick that Bruce and Valentina wrote off Luigi so quickly. *These are the last two people I would go into business with.*

After dinner, Nick ordered another bottle of champagne and the freshly made sorbet. The topic then returned to one of finances.

Bruce returned to his previous rant. "I need to get the money Luigi promised me to *Strut*," he whined.

"You need the money to *Strut*?" Nick asked. "I'm confused."

"*Strut* is the name of his agency in L.A.," Suzanne said.

"Another interesting agency name," Nick said.

"I'm content to stay at Luigi's home and see what pans out. But he promised me money—to cover my losses while I'm here and not working at the agency in Brazil," Valentina said.

"That sounds familiar," Suzanne said. "He promised all of us money."

Nick reached for his champagne and took a sip. The others did the same.

Valentina set her glass down first. "Of course, as I am a guest of Luigi's, I am honor-bound to tell him we talked about our concerns during dinner tonight," she said, dropping yet another bomb on the now-wilted flower centerpiece.

"The smoke is clearing," Nick said when he and Suzanne were back in the car with Massimo.

"I think so, too," Suzanne replied.

"So, why are we here?" Nick asked.

"Luigi is searching for a wife for the Emir, and that wife is Emma."

"That's what I think. Why do Bruce and Valentina feel pimping young girls to wealthy men is acceptable?"

"I don't know. I certainly don't think it's acceptable," Suzanne said.

"Everyone is out for themselves and they are desperate, and in my experience desperate people are dangerous," Nick said.

"Bruce has a third-rate agency in L.A. and where Valentina is in Brazil is not a top market," Suzanne said.

"What are we going to do?" Nick asked.

"I'm going to do everything in my power to make sure Emma has real work," Suzanne said, checking the time on her mobile phone. "It's ten in the morning in Honolulu. When we get back to the apartment, I'll give Emma a call."

In the loft, Suzanne called the home number for Emma Bedford. "I can't get through. The call keeps dropping."

"Here, use my phone," Nick said, handing it to her.

Suzanne dialed the number and listened. "It's going through. I'll put it on speaker."

Emma's mother answered the phone. "Hello Christine, this is Suzanne Langston calling from Milan."

"Did you get a new number? I don't recognize this one?"

"No, my phone won't dial out to Hawaii right now. I'm using the phone of my associate, Nick Thomas."

"Hello, Christine," Nick said.

"Hello. Suzanne, I want to know about the agency. What do you think of Luigi?"

"*swank* is not a good fit for Emma. I've been talking to other agencies here, trying to find a better place for her."

"I can't wait for you. I want Emma out modeling." She sounded whiney and irritated. "I want her to work in Australia or Europe. You said she'd be working soon. What about *swank*?"

"*swank* does not appear to be a modeling agency. They have little activity. I don't know what they do."

"Why can't she start at *swank*?"

Nick whispered to Suzanne, "May I give it a try?"

She gestured for him to go ahead.

"Christine, *swank* is not a place for Emma or anyone else who is serious about modeling. Suzanne is talking with the other agencies in town trying to get the best deal for Emma. She's generating a lot of interest."

"Well, I can't wait for Suzanne."

"By the end of the week, she will have scouted the land for Emma. You should wait until Suzanne finishes and we have more information to go on," Nick said.

"I want her working now."

TWENTY-THREE
WHY ARE YOU SPEAKING SICILIAN?

Nick rolled out of bed and on the way to the bath reviewed what he had heard at the dinner table the previous night. He had an odd dream he was sitting between Grace Kelly and Emma Bedford in the back seat of the Alfa Romeo as Massimo drove like a madman. They were trying to evade Luigi and Francesca who were following in Francesca's black Fiat. The mirrors on the Alfa Romeo were flipping in and out as they sped by the cars. At one time they were driving up the dry canals of the city.

He shook his head to clear the images. He took a bath then stood in front of the mirror and used soap and his grandfather's shaving brush to lather his face. When he finished shaving, he went into the salon with his journal and wrote about the previous day's events. It cleared his mind for the day ahead.

After journaling, and over coffee and biscuits, Nick and Suzanne discussed her contract with Luigi. They spent the rest of the morning writing an agreement to present to Luigi.

Massimo was waiting at the curb when they descended the stairs. They had a leisurely ride to *swank*, chatting with Massimo on the way, enjoying the comparison of culture and language.

At one point Massimo said, "It is not my business, but I do not understand what you are here to do."

Suzanne and Nick described the model center in Hawaii and explained how the current favorite location of South Beach in Miami was getting cliché. After the discussion the previous evening with Bruce and Valentina and her running off to tell Luigi about it, Nick was hesitant to divert from the "party line" with Massimo. He noticed it in Suzanne as well. For all Nick knew, Massimo may report back to Luigi about Suzanne and his discussions. Nick laughed to himself, thinking he was paranoid.

"That is what we are here to do," Nick summed up.

Massimo caught Nick's eyes in the rearview mirror.

"Is that what they want to do at *swank*?" he asked.

"It's what we came here for," Nick said.

"Oh."

"Do you know anything different?" Nick asked.

"No. But it is a strange business."

"You've got that right," Nick said *en sotto voce*, looking out the window at mid-morning Milano.

"*Pardon*?" Massimo said.

"Indeed. It is a strange business," Nick said.

The rest of the ride was in thoughtful silence.

As they entered the agency, Nick asked Suzanne. "Do you think we can trust him?"

"Massimo? I don't know who we can trust here," she replied.

In the elevator to the third floor, Nick took a whiff. "Luigi must be back from Switzerland. I can smell his cologne."

"Or it's Bruce. He wears the same fragrance."

"Yes, but he doesn't slather it on as Luigi does."

The elevator door opened, and they headed to the lobby.

"I want to print out the contracts, budgets, and schedules so we can go over them," Nick said, heading to Francesca's office.

Francesca saw Nick checking the printer's paper tray. "The printer has not worked for days, and the repairman won't be here until Friday."

Driving around the Hawaiian Islands in an English sports car repeating Italian tapes may seem like a multicultural experience, but it did not get Nick any closer to being able to troubleshoot a laser printer in Italy.

"Let's see what I can do. We've nothing to lose," Nick replied.

He turned the printer off, then unplugged it, waited a minute, plugged it back in, and turned it back on. Nick turned toward her to see the two bookers behind Francesca watching his process. He then opened his laptop, joined the office network, and found the printer was online. He opened a file, ran through the menu, and found *Stampa* in the menu. *That has to be 'Print'.* He clicked on it and the print menu came up, chose three pages, and then tapped the return key. A light on the printer blinked. Nick heard whispering behind him as the paper came out.

"Oh," Francesca said.

Nick checked the first page to emerge to see if it printed. There was a smattering of applause from behind him. Luigi poked his head into Francesca's office, drawn by the noise. Francesca, in rapid-fire Italian, gestured from Nick to the printer, tapping it a few times.

Luigi crossed his arms and leaned back against the doorjamb, staring at Nick. It was a pose to which he had become accustomed.

Gabriella came to Nick while he was reviewing his printouts.

"Nicholas, look at me," she said, handing him a copy of *Paris Match* opened to the society page. It seemed to Nick the entire magazine was filled with society pages. There was Gabriella, seated between a well-known financier and his supermodel girlfriend in a Monte Carlo hotel.

"Cool," Nick responded with a modicum of enthusiasm.

"Cool?"

"That's nice, Gabriella," Nick said. "When was the photograph taken?" He flipped the magazine to its cover.

"Three months ago."

Nick supposed there was a time when he was impressed by such things. He was more impressed by a musician's artistry than getting a great deal of money by inheritance and therefore having one's photograph placed in the society pages, something he was once accustomed to. Or the fact one's eyes, nose, lips, and cheekbones are set within the correct millimeter of one another to produce 'beauty'. Not that he didn't appreciate it when he saw it.

"That's nice, Gabriella," Nick said.

Gabriella was nonplussed by Nick's lackluster response.

He was saved by Luigi.

"I would like to talk to you now," he said, coming into the room.

Excusing himself from Gabriella, Nick made his way to Luigi's office.

"Take a seat. What is your name again?" Luigi asked.

The gambit was old and moronic and it bored Nick. He pulled out a card and flicked it across the table to Luigi without meeting his eye. The card bounced off his water glass and came to a rest in front of him.

"Suzanne should also be at this meeting," Nick said.

"Let's talk, the two of us." He paused. "How do you see our agreement?" Luigi asked.

"I am concerned with how things are coming together. Suzanne had expected to receive the rest of the funds when she arrived on Saturday as you promised, and here it is Wednesday and nothing has been wired to Honolulu."

Nick handed him a spreadsheet of Suzanne's expenses and a list of Luigi's agreed-upon payments.

He leaned forward and peered at it intently, running a pen down the column of numbers. He got up and went to the door, beckoning Francesca to join them. She came in, nodded hello to Nick, and stood behind Luigi while they reviewed the numbers together. Their conversation was in Italian. Nick sat back, trying to appear disinterested, but he focused carefully on their discussion, following along on his own copy. Most of what they said was numbers, which was the first lesson on his Italian tape, the pronunciation fine-tuned to Sicilian by Willie.

Nick interrupted their discussion to clarify a point. *"Mi scusassi, no, es cinquanta mille,"* he said, getting up and pointing to a number in the right-hand column. They both stopped, looked at each other, looked at him, and looked back at the paper.

"Si, cinquente mille," Francesca said, using her pen to cross out Luigi's number.

There was a pause and Luigi turned to Nick, his head cocked to one side. He stood staring at Nick, this time without arms akimbo. Nick was sure Luigi was wondering if he spoke Italian and then thought back to what Nick may have overheard.

"Why are you speaking Sicilian?" Luigi asked.

Nick shrugged his shoulders.

"May I make a copy of this?" Francesca asked in English.

"Of course," Nick said.

When Francesca left, Nick handed Luigi the contract that he had worked out for Suzanne. Luigi flipped through it.

"She is asking for too much money. Do you know how much a model scout makes?"

"Of course," Nick said. "And she is not even asking that of a top scout. I'm sure you would not have flown her across the world if you did not think she was worth the going rate. She is worth it, is she not?" Nick asked.

Nick was sure that Luigi would react strongly, and he did not disappoint.

"Suzanne must honor her commitment, and then she will receive the rest of the money," Luigi half yelled.

"I know of no commitment that Suzanne hasn't honored," Nick replied, keeping his voice even and low. He had long believed the first one to raise his voice in a negotiation had lost.

"Where is Emma?" Luigi yelled, his voice raising in pitch, his eyebrows growing bigger and more furious.

"Emma?" Nick asked.

"Emma Bedford. Where is Emma?" Luigi demanded, pounding his fist on the desk.

"I was under the understanding that the reason Suzanne is here is to get the organization up and running, as we discussed last night. If this is only about Emma, why didn't you mention her in our meeting last night or before we left Honolulu?" Nick asked.

Luigi waffled and squirmed, muttering in Italian. "Where is Emma?" he repeated in a high-pitched voice, pounding his fist on the desk.

It was a child's tantrum, and it took effort for Nick not to burst out laughing.

Growing up in a well-heeled and socially connected household in San Francisco, combined with his brief career in the world of aerospace, Nick spent a great deal of time knocking elbows with those in power. He found some were brilliant, some were complete idiots, some were easy to work with, some were bullies, some had humble beginnings, and some were born into wealth and power. They were a true cross-section of the country's population. He concluded from that experience that they were all just people. Once he realized that, he was not easily intimidated. To Nick, Luigi was nothing but a twerp, and no amount of yelling and pounding would get a rise out of Nick.

"I'll tell Suzanne you expect Emma to be here before you will pay her what you promised," Nick said, standing up, straightening his tie, and shooting his cuffs. He took in Luigi, who was still leaning forward from his rant, then turned and left him and his hawk nose and furious eyebrows alone in his office.

He walked to the back of the agency where Luigi had given Suzanne an office with a desk and a phone.

"We're making progress," Nick announced from the doorway.

"Oh?" she asked.

"I just got out of the talk with Luigi," he said, dropping into a chair beside the desk. "I told him you should be in the meeting, but he wanted the men to talk," Nick said, rolling his eyes.

"Italy. It hasn't changed much," Suzanne said.

"Whether you get paid depends upon whether Emma Bedford arrives in Milan. The entire deal hinges upon Emma making an appearance."

"What? This has nothing to do with Emma. This has to do with expanding modeling in Hawaii," Suzanne said.

"That is what I told Luigi."

"And his reaction?" she asked.

"Where is Emma?" Nick yelled in a high-pitched voice, pounding on the little desk in the little office. He did a fairly reasonable impression of the little Mussolini, he felt.

Suzanne's jaw dropped.

"It was funny, in its way."

"I don't find it funny."

"By funny, I mean odd. I gathered from our discussion with him yesterday he has done nothing regarding the development of his Hawaii business. Maybe now we have an idea of why we are here. He certainly does not want to pay you what you want for scouting. Did Luigi and you talk about Emma?"

"Only briefly. He gave me no indication he wanted her here with us."

"He wants her now."

"I'll go talk to him as if I don't understand what you discussed and see what I can come up with," she said, shaking her head.

With that, she left for Luigi's office.

Nick took *The Drifters* out of his attaché. It gave him a chance to get away from the noise and focus on something else.

In the book, George Fairbanks made his way to Torremolinos on the Costa del Sol of southern Spain. He was there to negotiate on behalf of his Swiss bank with a group of Greek shipowners. The Greeks had overextended themselves on the building of a huge apartment complex in the town.

They were meeting with Fairbanks to secure a loan; he was there to buy out their interest in the project.

As the negotiations continued, Fairbanks took the time to tour the town and get to know it better. There, he ran across some of the young people he knew from his earlier travels.

Nick stopped reading for a moment. Once, while touring Asia, he ran into the same group of travelers for the two months of the trip. They were all hitting the hotspots of different Asian countries, similar to what Fairbanks and the young people were experiencing.

After a while, he put the book away and walked out of the main booking room and sat, saying hello to the gang, acting as if nothing had gone on in the windowed office behind him. The bookers sat around reading newspapers and magazines. It was quiet and he could see Suzanne's back and her gestures through the window of Luigi's office. He caught Luigi's gaze through the window and held it until Luigi turned away.

Bruce came sweeping into the office.

"I am tired and this goddamn business of modeling has not changed in Italy in twenty years. I'm going home to my lover in L.A. I miss him."

Gabriella and Valentina rushed to him and patted him on the back and gave him hugs. He threw his arm back to his forehead and sobbed. The histrionics were Broadway-like, and could easily have been seen from the last row. The tragic floorshow continued until Bruce and Gabriella swept out the door as quickly as Bruce had swept in.

Suzanne's meeting with Luigi was a short one. She was out of his office and they were in Massimo's car heading to lunch.

"Hard day at work?" Massimo asked.

"Events have taken a strange turn," Nick said.

Massimo deposited them at *Ristorante Corte Santandrea* where Suzanne and Nick caucused. It was just the two of them for a change. Once in the restaurant, Daniel, the *maître d'*, approached the table.

"You are becoming my best customers," he said.

"Your food is excellent," Nick said.

They ordered, and when the waiter left, Nick filled Suzanne in on Bruce's meltdown and Gabriella's and Valentina's reactions.

"That's weird."

"With Luigi and Bruce both having hissy fits, that place is exhausting," Nick said. "Maybe it's that god-awful cologne they both wear."

Suzanne let out a laugh. "Perhaps."

"On another note, I followed through and called Luigi's bluff," Nick said, taking a sip of water.

"Luigi said that he resented you being here and that it was too early for you to be in on this deal," Suzanne said.

"What do you think?"

"I think I'm glad you're here," she replied.

"Based on our discussions, all I can figure is the whole Hawaii project is a ruse to get Emma here. You bringing me along has thrown a wrench into the proceedings as I am working toward making the Hawaii venture a reality."

"That's the only reason I'm here," Suzanne said.

"I get the impression Luigi wants your agency, but he can't figure out how to get it," Nick said.

"That's not going to happen."

A short time later, their food arrived.

"Let's not let the politics of business ruin a fine meal."

"I agree," Suzanne said.

"What are the plans for the cocktail party this evening?" Nick asked.

"I invited agency owners, bookers, models, and photographers."

"Are we through for the day?" Nick asked.

"I can't think of anything else we can accomplish. I'm at a loss for what to do next."

"Suzanne, I assume it is in your best interest to have Emma working in Milan?"

"I understand the direction you're heading. Sure, I'd like to have Emma working here. But I am extremely protective of my models and I want her to be working. I don't want to hear from her mother she was sold into white slavery, or whatever Luigi does."

"What would it take to make you comfortable with Emma coming here?" Nick asked, taking his notebook from his attaché.

"I'd want the basics any model going to Milan would get: a plane ticket, housing, a driver to take her to bookings, and a chaperone. I wouldn't let her on the plane without a defined promotion schedule. And if Luigi finds her to be such a hot property, the next top supermodel, I'd like her to have an advance for her work."

"Is an advance typical?"

"No, but it's not unheard of. One top model can make an

agency. If Luigi is convinced Emma is that model, you'd think he'd be willing to guarantee it."

"Can you shop her around the other agencies while we are in Milan? If she has serious potential, why waste her on a bozo like Luigi? Luigi brought us here to develop a Hawaii model business. If he doesn't want to talk about that, we can at least explore what we can do for Emma."

"It's an idea," Suzanne replied.

"Let's experience Milan and then sleep on it. Perhaps a new dawn will bring insight. Not to mention the aftermath of a good party."

They finished lunch with espresso and went back to *swank*. There they found Bruce newly shod in the finest Italian leather, wearing a designer cashmere sport coat and cashmere slacks. The astronomically expensive accouterments were gifts from Gabriella. It was how they spent their lunch hour. Bruce was now back to "normal" and smiling and talkative as if nothing had happened. Back in their little office, Nick asked Suzanne, "Do you think if I have a hissy fit in front of the office staff, Gabriella will update my wardrobe?"

"It's worth a try."

Nick was amused by the low drama, but getting bored with it. He wanted to see the sights, rub elbows with Italians, and experience how the city lives at its actual level, not at the make-believe business of *swank*.

"What do you say we *andiamo* out of this office and into Milan?" Nick suggested.

"That's a great idea."

They headed out the door into Massimo's Alfa Romeo.

"Massimo, please get us out of here," Nick asked him.

"Of course."

The next stop was at a supermarket for supplies for the party at the apartment that evening. They bought coffee and biscuits, wanting to replenish Natalie's supply. Nick always tried to stop at a local market when visiting a foreign country. It gave him an insight into how the locals live, and he enjoyed figuring out the unrecognizable things in the store. He tried out his Italian and was sure he mangled the tongue, but the shopkeepers seemed to appreciate his effort.

They bought cheese and crackers and a case of wine and headed back to the apartment.

Natalie's original idea was to have takeout Chinese and by the time Nick and Suzanne arrived, she had instead prepared a table full of exotic hors d'oeuvres. She outdid herself with a mix of Hawaiian, American, and Italian edibles. She had teriyaki chicken skewers, a pasta dish, an artichoke dip, and other tidbits.

"How can we dress up the table?" Natalie asked.

"I have just the thing," Nick said, heading up to the loft and retrieving a *pareo* from his suitcase he had brought as a gift in case he got to Greece to see his cousins.

"Here," he said, presenting it to Natalie, "Perhaps you can use this as a tablecloth."

Twenty-Four
I think it is a cultural thing

Nick, Suzanne, Natalie, and David were dressed for the party by nine o'clock when the guests began arriving. As the apartment began to fill, Nick surveyed the crowd. There were models, top photographers, agency owners and executives, a fashion magazine editor, and a few aspiring designers. Bruce and Valentina were also in attendance.

"Gabriella can't make it tonight. She sends her regards," Bruce said.

Nick made brief polite talk with them and left to mingle.

A few minutes later, Luigi arrived. Nick watched him survey the room with a look of awe at the power present.

Nick poured himself a glass of champagne and found himself talking with two bookers from *Salto!* agency in Milan. Laurance was French/German and Monika, a Peruvian/Italian who had lived in Los Angeles for six years. Laurance described herself as an ex-model who 'got out of the business in time'.

"What are you doing in Milan?" Laurance asked.

Nick told her about Suzanne hiring him to assist her in a project with *swank*.

"Ugh. *swank*. I have a friend who worked there as a booker for two days and then quit," Monika said.

"Why did she quit?" Nick asked.

"She was bored and said it wasn't a real agency and couldn't figure out what they did." She looked past Nick and waved. "Excuse me. Nice to meet you, Nick. Good luck with *swank*." She turned and walked across the room.

"Are you staying in Milan long?" Laurance asked.

"Probably just the week. The meetings are not going smoothly. I may have to travel straight back to Honolulu. May I get you a glass of champagne?" Nick offered.

"Please."

He went to the table and poured two glasses, and they resumed their discussion in a corner of the apartment.

"You are from countries other than Italy. Perhaps you can give me an overview of Italian business practices?" Nick asked.

She looked shocked. Nick was concerned.

"Is there something wrong?"

"It's odd for a man in this town to be asking a woman her opinion," she replied.

"I'm not from this town."

She thought for a moment and then said, "You are hard to place in the Italian hierarchy because of your clothes, the way you talk, and the way you hold yourself. Your clothes are timeless. They are not the fashion of the moment." Nick was dressed in what became his uniform of a blue blazer, gray slacks, white shirt, and tie. He wore polished Swiss shoes. "Italians look at a person starting with the shoes and then their eyes travel to the wristwatch and then to the rest. Then there's the direct eye contact, usually held longer by the women."

"I have already noticed the eye contact. It took me a while to become comfortable with it. What is it about, by the way?"

"I think it is a cultural thing," Laurance replied.

"Our negotiations with Luigi are not going well," Nick said.

"The Italians strive first to place a person on a socio-economic scale before they do business," she said. "He places you on an equal or higher footing with himself. His power has diminished in the negotiations and he isn't happy."

Nick glanced across the room. Luigi was standing with his back to a wall, out of place. He caught Nick's eyes, then looked away.

No, Luigi did not look happy. Nick decided to give him a wide berth that evening.

Laurance and Nick continued their discussion, which included international politics, culture, art, and language.

At eleven o'clock, she told Nick, "I have enjoyed talking with you. You should look me up when you are again in Italy. You can find me at *Salto!*"

"I'd like that."

"I need to go home now. I don't burn like that. I limit my all-night escapades to one night on the weekend, if that," she said.

Around midnight, Nick found himself in the kitchen playing a drinking game with three models who had wandered in fashionably late. Nick had read about the game in *On Her Majesty's Secret Service* by Ian Fleming. James Bond had tracked his arch-enemy to a chalet high in the Swiss Alps. There, as Bond would, he sat in a bar with six beautiful women with a desire to entertain them. Being the resourceful chap that he was, he took a champagne glass, wet the rim, placed a paper napkin on it, and placed a coin in the center of the napkin. Using cigarettes, everyone took turns burning tiny holes in the paper. The one that made the coin drop lost the game. The loser would have to buy the group a round of drinks. Here the champagne was flowing freely, and no one had to pay. Bond was a hit at the party, and so was Nick.

Having never been one to smoke, Nick felt as though he had inhaled the equivalent of a pack or two that night. Nick saw Italian paper napkins burned like a fuse for an incendiary device. *Was Ian Fleming aware of that?*

They were into the second round of the game when Suzanne poked her head into the kitchen. She saw Nick taking his turn at the glass, with three beautiful heads of hair next to his own. There was only a thread of napkin holding up the coin and the women watched his moves intently. Nick burned through the last bit of paper and let the coin drop, accompanied by squeals of delight and kisses on his cheek. He turned his head and saw Suzanne standing in the kitchen doorway, shaking her head and laughing. He winked at her.

The party ebbed at one-thirty and the last guest left shortly thereafter. Nick, Suzanne, Natalie, and David did a quick clean-up of the apartment. When they finished, Natalie came into the dining room from the kitchen.

"Look what I squirreled away in the back of the refrigerator," she said gleefully, showing them a bottle of Dom Pérignon.

Nick washed and dried four champagne flutes and brought them to the dining table.

They sat at the table and sipped and compared notes about the night.

"Nick enjoyed himself," Suzanne said.

"I noticed," Natalie and David said in unison.

"I really did," Nick agreed. Two of the models had handed him their email addresses and mobile numbers.

"I got a couple of modeling jobs," David said.

"And I have a magazine cover to shoot," added Natalie. She turned to Suzanne. "Thank you for coming up with the idea for a party."

"Yes, thank you," said David.

They sat drinking champagne and reflecting on the evening.

Natalie took another sip. "I asked Luigi about his parents. I told him I recognized his name," she said. "He told me he was from a prominent legal family in Rome. He said he gets down there to visit when he can."

"He told me his parents were dead," Suzanne said.

Nick took another sip. *Dom Pérignon still tastes dusty to me.*

TWENTY-FIVE
NICK SLID AWAY FROM THE RUCKUS

It was late the next morning when Suzanne and Nick gathered at the breakfast table for coffee and biscuits.

"Luigi told me last night at the party he was going to Switzerland again today," Suzanne said.

"I wonder if that is what he is really doing?" Nick said.

"Who knows what he is up to?"

Nick took a sip of coffee. "I guess it doesn't matter at this point, but let's play this out. Perhaps we can salvage something after all."

"I would like to take the day to make inroads and reunite with more agencies in town. I have models I would like to place," Suzanne said.

"You might as well make good use of the downtime."

"It's late. Why don't we grab lunch and go from there?"

David and Natalie joined Suzanne and Nick for lunch at a café near the apartment, and then the four caught a tram for *Salto!*

The agency offices were in an elegant old apartment. When they walked in the door, Nick saw his new friends Laurance and Monika hard at work. Laurance's office was in what had once been a dining room with French doors and polished wood floors. The place was hopping, and they had little time to talk. When they saw him, they jumped up, kissed him on the cheek, and went back to work answering phones and working on their computers.

Natalie, Suzanne, and Nick parted with David and continued to the *Stile Agency*, where Suzanne and Nick met with the owner, Alessandro. Alessandro's own office was furnished with red leather chairs, a fireplace, and high ceilings with a Latin prayer around the top molding. There were numerous framed pictures of his young son on the walls. Suzanne took the opportunity to inquire about Luigi.

"Ah, Luigi. Yes, I know of him."

"Have you done business with him?" Suzanne asked.

"Me? No. But I suppose some people do. I can't say I know of any."

"Is *swank* a good agency?"

"I don't know what that agency does," he said.

Suzanne gave up asking about Luigi and showed Alessandro a photo of Tessa, a Greek girl whom she wanted to meet with in Paris.

"She's fabulous. How old is she?" he asked, taking the photo and examining it.

"Thirteen."

"Ack. By the time she is eighteen, she could have the face of a monster," he said.

While Suzanne continued agency hopping, Natalie went back to the apartment. David and Nick made their way to view Leonardo da Vinci's mural, *The Last Supper*.

"How did you end up in Italy?" Nick asked David.

"I kind of fell into it. I was teaching tennis at a country club in Connecticut near my parents' home. One of my clients suggested I try modeling. She called a friend in Italy and the next thing I knew, I was on a plane. A month later, I met Natalie, who was photographing a campaign for an Italian department store."

"So how do you like modeling in Milan?" Nick asked as they walked.

"I won't do what it takes to get booked for the bigger modeling assignments here," he said, deftly sidestepping a fortyish woman who stopped in her tracks in front of David to ogle him.

"What does that entail?" Nick asked.

"It means sleeping with the appropriate people," he replied.

"Ah."

"Of any sex," he added.

Nick and David arrived at *Santa Maria della Grazie* and *Cenacolo Vinciano*, the refectory next to the church. The place was like a bank vault. They walked through a door and into a room with another door. Then the door in front of them opened only after the door behind them closed. They went through that process three times before they got into the chapel.

"The Italians take their national treasures seriously," David said.

Nick was shocked to see that a doorway was cut into the base of the mural. The painting was faded and there were patches of restored areas. Leonardo used a homemade pigment that deteriorated the moment he completed the mural and by the time the door was installed in the 1600s, it was already nearly unrecognizable. The refectory was also used as an armory and a stable. In World War II, a bomb hit it. It had gone through so many restorations there was not much of the original painting left to view. A woman was sitting on a ladder working on restoring a small section.

Nick was glad he saw the mural and took a picture without using the flash in deference to the posted rules. As he stood admiring what was left of the master's work, a woman walked up beside him and took a flash picture of the supping prophet. You would have thought another bomb hit the quiet chapel. In seconds, she was surrounded by guards and docents haranguing her in Italian. When that didn't work, they switched to English and French. When she finally responded in German, two of the five switched to that language and the discussion grew louder.

Nick slid away from the ruckus.

They left the battle at *The Last Supper* and took a long walk to *La Gioia* model agency. David was signed with *La Gioia* and needed to check in. The agency was in one of the most beautiful buildings Nick had seen in Milan. Made of stone, marble, and brass, it had an aviary in the courtyard. Like the other agencies they had been to, this one was in high gear and models flowed in and out the front door.

Nick reached for the handle and was knocked to the ground by a woman as she blasted out the front door. Nick recognized her from the cover of a magazine he had seen at one of the agencies but didn't know her by name. She apologized, reached down, hauled him to his feet, and disappeared.

After David checked in and they visited with a couple of models in the lobby, they walked home, taking in the street life of Milano on the way.

Back at the apartment, Nick helped Natalie make dinner of chicken cacciatore. And after dinner, David and Nick went for gelato, a few blocks from the apartment. David and Natalie said there was much better in town, but Nick couldn't imagine how that could be.

Nick and Suzanne sat in the salon after dinner.

"So what is Emma Bedford like, by the way?" Nick asked.

"Long legs, tall, blonde, beautiful. According to my other models, she runs with a bad crowd. She's still in high school and dates a lot of guys in their thirties."

"She should fit right in here," Nick said.

"She just might."

"High school? How old is she?" he asked.

"Seventeen."

Nick thought of the beautiful Greek girl, Tessa, whose photo Suzanne showed to Alessandro.

"Isn't Emma a little over the hill to be getting into this business?"

Twenty-Six
Emma Bedford

Emma Bedford grew up attending a Catholic school on the Windward side of Oahu. When she was ten years old, her life changed when her mother divorced, quickly remarried, and had another child. Her mother poured her attention into her new family and left Emma to fend for herself.

Like many school girls her age, Emma was fond of selfies and rebellion. Being beautiful and tall—she was 5' 10" at fourteen—she attracted the attention of older men. She could pass for a woman in her twenties and often did. She liked men in their thirties and older with jobs and the means to take her places and buy her things.

Emma started skipping school, and when her mother got the word, she was happy to avoid the private school tuition and sent Emma to a nearby public school. Compared to Catholic school, the curriculum required little effort on Emma's part, and she put in the minimum. She spent a lot of time at the beach, which is where Suzanne met and scouted her. With Emma being a minor, her mother was thrilled her daughter could bring in money and have something to do other than get into trouble. She was pregnant again and wanted to focus on her new family. She signed Emma's modeling contract.

Twenty-Seven
The last thing Hoffstetter wanted

Back in Switzerland, Julian Hoffstetter mulled over another request from Gabriella for money for the *swank* agency.

The word around Milan was Luigi Donati's aggressive approach to finding talent for *swank* alienated nearly all the agencies in Milan, and he was working his way through Paris.

He also heard Donati was a hothead with ties to the local crime syndicate. The last thing Hoffstetter wanted was to be involved with the *'Ndrangheta* or the Calabrian Mafia, which does business in most of Italy and a good part of the world.

He picked up a telephone and dialed.

It was time for Gabriella to come back to Switzerland.

TWENTY-EIGHT
JUST MAKING FRIENDS

"We will go to the *prêt-à-porter* shows today," Suzanne said. It had been a rare early night, and they slept long and were rested for the day ahead.

Later that morning at *swank*, Suzanne went to talk to Luigi and Nick hung back in the lobby as the lunch hour was approaching.

Out the glass front door, Nick saw young girls walking past the agency and down the hall.

Massimo came in and sat on the couch beside him.

"Luigi is from a powerful legal family in Rome," he offered.

"I have worked with powerful people before," Nick said. *He had to assume Massimo was in the 'enemy camp'.*

"No. No," he said in a lighter tone. "Luigi knows my friend and business partner in Turino. That's how I got this job."

"It's much the same in Hawaii. If I want to get consulting work, I need to have connections," Nick said.

There was a lull in the discussion.

"Are you part of this? Whatever this is?"

"No. No. And I do not like what I see," Massimo replied, holding Nick's gaze.

"Suzanne and I can trust you?" Nick asked.

"I will do nothing to harm you."

They studied each other intently.

"I believe you." And he did. Nick offered him his hand to shake. He took it in a firm grasp.

"We are dealing with very odd people, Massimo."

"Yes, Nicholas, we are."

Massimo drove them to the *Fiere Convention Center* for the *prêt-à-porter* shows.

"Suzanne asked Luigi to get you a pass. You can valet park the car and come in with us," Nick told Massimo.

They were admitted through the door, and the guard at the door scrutinized their passes.

The building was one of the ugliest structures Nick had seen in Italy. It resembled a blocky industrial warehouse made of cement. However, once inside, the place was amazing to walk around. It all had to do with the contents of the building: beautiful people in beautiful clothes. They passed dozens of camera crews interviewing designers and models as they made their way to the second-floor café.

"They are so tall. So tall and *bellissima*," Massimo said. "And they are all carrying bottles of water."

"Model bottles," Nick said.

Massimo turned to Suzanne. "I can't thank you enough for getting me a pass."

"You're quite welcome."

Massimo's head was snapping back and forth, taking it all in, a smile on his face.

Nick headed with Suzanne deeper into the building, Massimo following behind at a distance, head still snapping back and forth.

"You and Massimo are becoming chummy," Suzanne said.

"I believe him to be a good man and perhaps our only ally in Milan," Nick replied. "Here's an empty table. If you camp out here, I'll fetch some coffee."

"Thank you." She set herself down at a tiny nightclub-type table with Massimo.

Nick set off for the coffee bar at the other side of the room, winding his way through the crowd of tables filled with the fashion elite. The line was long and he took a spot at the end directly behind a couple. The woman was elegant, polished, and refined; the gentleman, dressed to the nines, fit the same bill.

"*Come stai oggi?*" she asked, turning to Nick.

"*Me excuse. Parlo un poco Italiano,*" he replied.

"I was asking how you are today," she said, switching to an English accent. She looked Nick up and down in that Italian way.

"That, I understood. I'm fine, thank you. How are you?"

"I'm fine. You look familiar. Have we met? You are Swiss?"

Her companion had turned, awaiting Nick's answer.

"Nicholas Thomas," he said, extending his hand. "I am American and I would have remembered you had we met before." It was an understatement. The woman oozed power and money and position.

"How charming you are. My name is Madeline Smithe. This is Geoffrey Haines." They shook hands all around.

"What brings you to Milan, Mr. Thomas?"

"Nicholas, please. You know we Americans and our informality."

"In that case, I am Maddie and this is Geoff," she said.

"Ostensibly, I am here with a client to set up an international modeling agency with an Italian company. But now that I am here, I don't know what our Italian colleagues have in mind," Nick told them.

"Ah, welcome to Italy!" Geoff offered. "From where do you hail?"

"Honolulu."

"Hawaii! How delightful!" Maddie replied. "You are a long way from home. We came over from London for the shows."

"Are you in the business?" Nick asked.

There was a silent look between them.

"Maddie is the publisher of some of the more influential fashion magazines," Geoff said.

"Ah. Well, then it must be obvious I am a rank amateur in this business," Nick admitted.

"That's refreshing," Maddie said.

The line moved forward, and Geoff placed an order for an espresso and cappuccino. The barista asked Nick for his order. "*Tre cappuccino*," Nick said.

"Why three?" Maddie asked.

"One for my client and me, one for our driver."

"Your driver? Good for you. People count," Maddie said.

"They do indeed," Geoff concurred.

"I've always believed that," Nick agreed.

By then they had their hands full, Nick himself juggling three hot cups.

Maddie took a business card from her attaché. She handed Geoff her cup so she could write on the back of the card.

"Here is our number. If you need any help in your dealings with the Italians, please call. This town can be difficult for the outsider." She slid the card into his breast pocket.

"I'm most grateful," Nick said.

"It was a pleasure meeting you," Maddie said.

"I feel the same. I'll see you around Milan, I'm sure." Nick replied.

They parted company, and Nick headed back to Suzanne and Massimo with the coffee.

"Did you run into old friends?" she asked.

"No, new friends," Nick said, handing her Maddie's card. She took it and he watched with amusement as her eyes got big.

"Maddie said I could call if I needed help with the Italians. She and Geoff should be here through the weekend."

"Geoff?"

"Geoffrey Haines," Nick said, retrieving Maddie's card and examining it. It was a simple card, as the more powerful ones tend to be.

Massimo gestured at the cappuccino. "*Grazie*, Nicholas," he said, reaching for his wallet.

Nick waved him off and joined them at the table. They made idle chitchat and watched the parade of models pass by while they drank their coffee.

After a while, Nick excused himself and left the two of them in search of a restroom. The way was marked with an enormous sign above a curtain proclaiming *TOILETTE* ⬇. He followed the sign and walked behind a curtain revealing stairs to the left and a passage to the right. Following the passage into the bowels of the building through corridors and down concrete passageways, he walked for almost five minutes, thinking he must've made a wrong turn. Electrical cable trays and pipes hung overhead, yet there was no other way to go. Nick continued and heard voices ahead. Poking his head around a corner, he was greeted with laughter from a crowd of people. The building had claimed another victim.

One model, whom he recognized, called out, "Are you searching for the toilet, too?"

Nick shrugged and nodded, "I take it I am not the only one?" He counted nine, including himself.

A famous designer emerged from around the corner. "There is nothing back there but the end of the passage and a maintenance area."

They knew each other and introduced themselves to Nick.

There was no pretense among these icons of their industry, all in need of relief.

They walked another five minutes back to the main floor, encountering another dead end before pouring out through the curtain. It was an odd bonding experience filled with laughter.

Suzanne walked up to Nick at that point.

"Don't go that way," Nick said, pointing to the big *TOILETTE* sign above their heads. His comment was met with an uproar of laughter by designers, models, and editors alike. Nick introduced Suzanne to the few in the crowd she didn't know.

"I still really have to pee," announced one model. The crowd nodded in agreement. They shook hands, hugged, did the Italian kiss-kiss thing, and went their separate ways.

"The first one to find it yell," someone called from the distance.

"What was that about?" Suzanne asked.

"Just making friends," he replied.

Suzanne and Nick parted company. She had a pass for the shows. Massimo and Nick had them only for the antics in the halls. Massimo's head was still snapping back and forth, taking in the beautiful women.

"*Grazie*, Nicholas, *Grazie*," he kept repeating.

If Massimo wasn't on our side before, he is now, Nick thought.

When they finished their coffee, Nick said, "Let's take a walk."

They got up and headed down the hall, hearing music and applause behind the guarded doors. Nick ran into a few of the crowd from his search for the restroom and later Maddie and Geoff.

"How do you know all of these people? You really do work in this modeling business, don't you?" Massimo asked.

"No, I really don't. I just make friends quickly."

A while later, Massimo continued on his tour and Nick

returned to the café. The late nights were taking a toll, and he wanted more coffee. As he was walking to the line, he fell in behind a woman, impeccably dressed, dark hair ending in the middle of her back. As she walked, she caught the heel of her shoe on an uneven spot on the floor. In what resembled a ballet or judo move, she spun as she fell. Nick caught her eyes for a moment as she careened into him and took him to the floor with her. Twice in the last twenty-four hours, he had been knocked to the floor. Nick lay on his back with a woman looking into his eyes.

She was on top of him.

She smelled wonderful.

Twenty-Nine

Lazuli Árnadóttir

"I feel as though we should introduce ourselves," Nick said, taking in the deepest blue eyes he had ever beheld.

She got up quickly and pulled Nick to his feet. She had a lovely grip, and she held his hand for a moment as she said, "Lazuli Árnadóttir."

They looked around. Their tumble didn't gather attention.

"Nicholas Thomas."

"I owe you at least a cup of coffee." Her accent was partly English, partly unspecific European, and delicious.

They took their coffee to a table. It struck Nick that hers was a classic beauty, the type that makes a man ache down deep, where he can't do anything about it. Every element of her was in perfect proportion. She wore minimal makeup and had a sparkle in her eyes. She sat upright in her chair, her posture confident, her manner serene.

He couldn't take his eyes off her.

"You have a fascinating name," Nick said. "I've not met a Lazuli before."

"My father loves the gemstone Lapis Lazuli and loves the color blue."

"It's very attractive," Nick said, gesturing to her ring.

She looked down at her finger. "Lapis has been mined since the seventh millennium BC in Afghanistan. It was even in the funeral mask of Tutankhamun. Some of the finest Renaissance painters, like Titian and Vermeer, used ground-up Lapis Lazuli in their blue paint—their ultramarine blue."

"Is it only found in Afghanistan?" Nick asked, intrigued by her passion for the subject.

"It's also found in Iran, Russia, Peru, Pakistan, Italy, and even in the US and Canada. I have seen enough that I can tell the difference. Persian and Afghani Lapis are the finest with little pyrite—that's the gold specs you sometimes see, and it has no calcite. That's the white you often see in Lapis. The Russian or Siberian has pyrite and calcite. The Peruvian may have a green color and lots of calcite. Then there is the fake stuff—the synthetics. Some are cheap dyed howlite or sodalite or something else."

She paused her dissertation, took a breath, and waited for Nick's reaction.

"Well, I think it's fascinating," Nick said, "and your eyes light up when you talk about it." He took a sip of coffee.

"I've become somewhat of an expert on Lapis Lazuli," she said sheepishly.

"Do you have much?" Nick asked.

She touched her ring. "Besides this, I have bracelets and necklaces and earrings. I also have loose stones I have collected. This ring is high quality." She slipped it off her finger and handed it to Nick.

He examined it. It was a solid dark blue color, with no gold pyrite specs or white calcite. He handed the ring back to her.

"I adore Lapis Lazuli. It's a good thing, I suppose," she said, taking the ring from him and putting it back on her finger.

"Yes, I think it is a good thing. Your ring is beautiful," Nick said.

"I don't wear it often. Lapis is a soft stone and not very durable and I can be clumsy. It's better suited for necklaces and earrings."

"Lazuli is a pretty name."

"Lazuli means sky or heaven. *Azul* is the root for blue in many languages.

"I'm called Skye, or *Blue* by friends and family. Sometimes *Azul*, by my brother, and *Zul* when we are arguing. My family likes to mix it up."

"What may I call you?" Nick asked.

She cocked her head. He smiled at her.

"You may call me Skye."

"And your last name? Árnadóttir?" Nick asked.

"Good memory."

"I'm good with names."

"What language is that?" Nick asked.

"I am an *Íslendingar*," she said, finally picking up her coffee and taking a sip.

"Iceland. I could not place your accent," Nick said.

"I was born in Iceland, but my parents immigrated to Sweden. I went to boarding school in England, so my accent is hard to place."

"So, Skye. What are you doing in Milan? Are you in the business?" Nick asked.

"I'm finishing my master's degree in international business at the Sorbonne. I took a year off to study the fashion industry for my degree, but I can't take it seriously. I got into it for the experience. I'll be going back to school next year," she said.

"I spent a year at the Sorbonne," Nick said.

That led to a discussion of the school, teachers they had in common, and where they lived in Paris.

"After university, I guess I'll go work for my father's company," Skye said with a sigh. And what about you?"

Nick gave her what was becoming his pat answer. He had learned distancing himself from the fashion industry increased his credibility in Milan. It was odd how no one wanted to spend time with their colleagues.

"So I am new to this business. It is not a typical engagement for me," Nick concluded.

"Yes, I can imagine," she replied. She leaned forward confidentially, giving him a whiff of her wonderful scent. It was crisp and clean, like fresh snow.

"Tell me, what do you think of this industry now that you have been in it for a week?" she asked.

Their eyes met. Hers were playful and bright. Okay, Nick thought. I'll give it to her straight.

"I think it's an industry of symbiotic prima donnas. Everyone needs everyone else: designers need photographers, photographers need fashion magazines, and the magazines need outrageous designers. From a business standpoint, I am still intrigued by where the money goes. Who buys this stuff? Are there that many people buying designer underwear for a hundred dollars a pop?"

"A pop?" she tossed her head back in laughter.

"Sorry for the idiom. One hundred dollars a pair. At any rate, I understand how photographers, models, and magazines make money. I'm not so sure about the designers."

"Your assessment is not far off, and the answer is yes. People are buying that much one-hundred-dollar underwear," Skye replied. "I'll send you a copy of my master's thesis and you can read all about it."

"I'd like that. Do you miss school?" Nick asked.

"I do. I would like to continue and study architecture. That does not fit into my father's plans for me."

"I'd like to hear how it works out for you." *This was one incredible woman. Too bad I leave in a couple of days.*

Then they really talked. They talked non-stop about art, literature, the fashion industry, of course, graduate school, life, love, and happiness. They volleyed back and forth, their eyes focused on each other the entire time. They laughed a lot. Skye's family had a textile concern in the family portfolio, and the fashion industry would have been a good fit.

It was obvious to Nick she came from a wealthy family. She was also intelligent and charming. In the forty-five minutes they talked, he was smitten.

She checked her watch. "Oh, my," she said. "I have to go. It was a great pleasure talking with you, Nicholas."

He stood with her. "Thank you for the coffee."

"Thank you for breaking my fall." She kissed him on both cheeks and spun around and walked away.

Nick was crestfallen as he watched her disappear into the throng.

A moment later, Massimo appeared at his elbow.

"Ready to go?" he asked.

"Yes, I suppose," Nick said.

"I saw you talking to that girl. She is really beautiful, even with all these models around us. Is she a new friend?"

"I hope so," Nick said, "but we didn't exchange numbers or anything, so probably not."

After one more tour of the floor and stepping around the paparazzi, Massimo and Nick left for American Express for cash. Nick bought him lunch at a corner café near *swank*.

It was a good time, the guys out on the town, driving around, taking in the sights, looking at the models.

"Who is on the stereo?" Nick asked.

"Laura Pausini. She sings in Italian, English, and Spanish," Massimo said.

"I'll have to find some of her music."

Later, they met Suzanne at *swank*.

"I'm starving," she said when she got in the car.

"We know just the place," Nick said. They headed back to the corner pub.

While Suzanne ate, they talked about the business proceedings.

"I'm getting tired of this. I'm bored with the negotiations and the speed at which we are progressing. Or not progressing. This is taking too long, and it's going nowhere," Suzanne said.

"Suzanne, by accident or design, this entire trip is about Emma. I'm sure this afternoon's meeting will be the same. There will be a lot of pressure to get Emma here."

"You're probably right," she said.

Massimo sat sipping his coffee and listening.

THIRTY

THE CHAMPAGNE FLOWED

Massimo dropped them off at the apartment, and they took naps to be fresh for the *beLLeZZa* party at nine o'clock that evening.

The invitation requested 'exotic black tie', and the four of them spent an hour dressing. Nick chose gray slacks and a blue blazer, his most formal attire. When they were getting ready, the women ran around the apartment in various forms of undress. To Nick's amusement, David repeatedly asked Natalie to put a top on over her black lacy bra. There was photographic evidence of both him and Natalie in the buff on the walls of the apartment. If Nick or anyone else wanted to see her even less attired, all they had to do was take in the photos on the walls.

She was proud of her breast implants and asked Nick what he thought of them. Nick surveyed the peaks. They were quite buoyant and defied gravity. However, they did not look as though they belonged where they were. But the lass was cheerfully displaying them for him, and he felt compelled to give a positive response.

"Impressive. Very nice indeed," Nick replied.

Assembled in their best duds, they taxied to *La Gare* nightclub and secured a booth near the action. Nick's choice of attire turned out to be fine; he was even overdressed. The place was painted black and red, with hundreds of fresh, long-stemmed red roses hanging from the ceiling. Nick scanned the room and saw lots of models and paparazzi. He waved to a few people he had met throughout the week.

The main table had a dozen Scandinavian models sitting as if on display. To Nick, it seemed their legs stopped at their chins. Suzanne talked with them while David and Nick made friends with the models at the buffet table. Anorexia was waning in Milan and the women were going for the food.

Back at the table, Suzanne introduced Nick to a fellow sailor, Georgio, who owned resorts in Sardinia and elsewhere. He was a family man, the most normal person Nick had yet met in Milan. Georgio had been in Hawaii recently and he and Nick bonded by talking about boats and sailing. He seemed as out of place in Milan as Nick did.

The champagne flowed, and after a while, Nick excused himself and made his way to the restroom. He walked through the main door. The bath had separate fully enclosed stalls and a unisex sink outside them. Nick saw a stall door ajar and walked in. A cover girl was in a stage of undress. Nick recognized her, but models had so many distinct looks, sometimes it was hard for him know who she was.

"Excuse me," Nick apologized, turning to go.

"Don't go. I'm nearly done and ready to leave," she replied. She seemed nice. She sure looked nice.

She turned her back and lifted her hair. "Do you mind?" she asked. Nick leaned forward and closed her zipper.

"I don't mind at all," he replied.

"You're an American," she stated.

"I am."

They went through the "Who are you? Where are you from?

What are you doing here?" dance. In the end, Nick made another friend. Claire was intelligent, humorous, and breathtakingly beautiful.

There were few things Nick enjoyed more than being deposited in a crowd where he didn't know anyone. He looked around. Suzanne was in deep discussion with a man on the other side of the room. Natalie and David were in conversation nearby. He set off into the room to rub elbows with the A-listers.

It was not long before he came across Maddie and Geoff.

"Nicholas," Maddie called. She waved him in her direction.

Nick gave a wave and made his way through the crowd.

"Good evening," Nick said.

"How goes the business with the Italians?" Geoff asked discretely.

"I believe it is over. We reached a stalemate. Our friend Luigi wanted much more than was reasonable. It got nasty," he said.

"That happens a lot in this business," Maddie said.

A moment later, he felt a hand on his shoulder. "I am bored with this modeling talk," Claire said in his ear. She turned to his companions. "Hello Maddie, Geoff. May I borrow Nicholas?"

"Of course. See you tomorrow, Claire," Maddie said. Nick shrugged as if to say, "What can I do?"

Claire took the champagne flute from his hand, finished the glass, and deposited it on the nearby bar. "For someone new to this business, you sure know the right people," Claire said.

"Yes, I can see being in your company has increased my stock immeasurably," he said, noting the attention leveled at Claire and then turned to him.

There were whispered discussions. *Who is he?*

The dance floor was accessible through a single door at the side of the bar. One would not know there was a cavernous room behind it unless one was dragged through the door. Nick was dragged through it by Claire. The music assaulted them when they entered.

They danced for a couple of songs. She was a remarkable and sensuous dancer, and her eyes flirted as she moved about the floor. In the middle of their fourth dance, he was cut in on. Claire shrugged her shoulders as she was pulled away. Nick stopped dancing and extended his lower lip. She pulled away from her new partner and planted a tremendous kiss on Nick's lips, instantly wiping away his pout.

Claire danced off; Nick danced on. He spun around and there was Suzanne, shaking her head. They were in a big circle of models bopping away.

Suzanne did not dance unnoticed, however. A pretty girl next to her danced up and bumped hips with her. It was one of those 1970s disco moves. The woman leaned in to talk to Suzanne. Nick saw Suzanne shake her head in response. The girl glanced at Nick and danced off. After a dance or two, Suzanne made a drinking gesture–tipping up an imaginary glass–and motioned to the bar.

They danced their way through the crowd to the bar. At 10 euros apiece for water, they decided on margaritas for the same price.

"*Due Margaritas!*" Nick yelled to the barkeep over the blaring music.

"*Due Margaritas!*" he shouted back.

The bartender did an elaborate lambada to the beat while mixing their drinks.

"She wanted to take me home with her," Suzanne said.

"Excuse me?"

"The woman on the dance floor—she wanted to take me home with her."

Nick scanned the room. The people on the dance floor looked like they were fornicating standing up. "Of course," he replied.

The bartender set down the drinks with a flourish. Nick handed one to Suzanne and they headed across the dance floor. Not far from the bar, the plastic cup holding Nick's Margarita cracked, and the drink began to pour down the front of him. Nick up-ended the drink and downed it in one gulp. Suzanne chose that time to look back and see if Nick was still behind her. Her eyes got big.

It was too loud for him to explain.

With his cup empty, they made their way out the door of the dance floor and back into the bar. Fabio, the head of the *FIG* agency in Paris, asked Suzanne to dance. She followed him to the dance floor and Nick directed himself to the bar to buy water to wash down the margarita. While he waited, he surveyed the crowd. It showed no signs of thinning, and he was joined by two model types.

"*Mi excuse,*" one said, knocking into him.

"That's quite all right," Nick said in English.

"You're an American. Hi, I'm Sandra. This is Sophia," she said.

"It's a pleasure to meet you."

"Where are you from in the states?" Sophia asked, leaning across Sandra to pay the bartender for the water.

"Honolulu."

"Honolulu? As in Hawaii? You are very far from home."

Sandra's friend Sophia was a native of Italy, and after doing the "Who are you and what are you doing here" thing, the three of them headed to the dance floor. It was approaching two a.m. and the dancing got obscene. Nick was the meat in the

Sandra/Sophia sandwich. After a few songs, they dragged him to the edge of the dance floor.

"Come home with us," Sophia pleaded.

"Yes, please do," Sandra said.

Across the room, Nick saw Maddie waving to catch his eye. No. Her head shook vehemently.

Nick turned to Sandra and Sophia, and then back at Maddie, who continued to shake her head no.

"I'm sorry ladies, as much as I'd enjoy the romp, I'm with someone this evening," Nick replied.

"Bring her along," they said in unison.

"No, I'm afraid that wouldn't do."

"Oh," Sandra said.

"We've never been turned down before," Sophia said.

"I have no trouble believing that," Nick said.

"Oh, well," Sophia said. They both kissed him on each cheek and moved like panthers onto the dance floor, in pursuit of new prey.

Nick made his way to Maddie. "You're up late," he said.

"I see Sandra and Sophia found you."

"Yes. But I'm afraid they'll have to find another target. Thank you for the save."

"I'm glad you heeded my advice," Maddie said. "I'm going to call it a night. These parties haven't changed much."

They said their goodbyes, and Maddie left through the front door, while Nick made his way to the side of the dance floor.

Suzanne reappeared, face flushed from dancing.

"I'm ready to go. How about you?" Suzanne asked.

"I believe I've experienced most of Milano," Nick said.

As they were leaving, he saw his friends Sandra and Sophia. They had a terrified guy pinned to the wall by the entrance. Perhaps Maddie had also warned him off, Nick thought.

THIRTY-ONE
You've got to see this

It was quiet at breakfast. Nick sat sipping coffee at the table with his fellow apartment dwellers. It was a long night, and four and a half hours of sleep were not nearly enough.

"You look a bit the worse for wear," Natalie said, putting a cool hand on his forehead.

"I feel hung over. I have a headache, and a sour stomach, and I'm achy. All I had last night was a glass of wine, a glass of champagne, and a margarita. I never even felt the effects of the alcohol."

"You're hungover," the crowd sang in unison.

"You're probably dehydrated," Natalie said.

"I'll have to sew one of those model bottles into my blazer and get a long straw," Nick said.

Later that morning, Natalie, David, Suzanne, and Nick went to a café for brunch. Lots of models were there, too. Milan was saturated with tall, beautiful people. While they were waiting to be seated, Nick saw a woman wearing a t-shirt with the logo of *Incognito*, a jazz-funk band from London.

"Great music, *Incognito* makes," Nick told her.

"You've heard of the band? Everyone here thinks I'm trying to hide," she said in a Jamaican accent.

Across the room, Cash from *FIG* waved a friendly hello. All towns get small once one is in them for a while, Nick reflected.

After being fortified at lunch and ready to move, they made a stop at *Teatro alla Scala*, the opera house known as *La Scala*.

While Natalie, David, and Suzanne sat in the sun watching the people on the piazza moving between the nearby museums, Nick entered the *La Scala*.

Inaugurated in 1778, *La Scala* replaced an older opera house that burned down during a party. Opera houses of the time were also casinos and used for trading and selling everything from livestock to equities, often drowning out the operas being performed.

Nick walked around the opera hall and made his way through the museum. *La Scala,* steeped in history, was stunning and powerful. Nick stood on a balcony and took in the grandeur, thinking of the music which had played there.

The scene reminded him of going to the opera *Carmen* with a girlfriend when he lived in San Francisco. The tickets were from her ex-boyfriend and when they arrived at the theater, they found their seats were far apart in different rows. During the more than three-hour performance, Nick realized the tickets were an impressive show of passive aggression on the part of the ex-boyfriend.

On the way back out to the street, he ran into a Japanese family blocking the stairwell taking pictures.

"*Mi excuse,*" Nick said, trying to get by.

A blank look.

"Pardon me."

Nothing.

"*Suememasen,*" he finally said, reverting to their native tongue.

"*Ah, so desu ne,*" the boy replied. The entire family bowed at the waist. Nick gave a quick bow and slid by. Behind him was an eruption of Japanese at high volume.

The next stop was the *Galleria de Vittorio Emanuele II,*

Italy's oldest shopping arcade, built a hundred years after *La Scala*. Known by locals as *Milan's drawing room—l salotto di Milano*—the galleria is a popular meeting and dining locale for the Milanese. The structure is four stories high and enclosed by a cast iron and glass-domed roof.

Nick took out his mobile phone and took pictures of the shops and the domed ceiling. He then stopped in various shops and bought fountain pen ink for himself, Italian coffee for Willie, and nougat candy for Nigel, known for his sweet tooth.

When they finished shopping, David said, "You've got to see this."

The four of them stood off to the side and watched a half dozen people. Tittering girls and macho Italian men walked up to a point on the floor and stopped and spun in place. As Nick got closer, he saw there was an inlaid mosaic of a bull on the floor.

He turned to David for an explanation.

"If you stop and twirl with the heel of your shoe three times on the testicles of the bull, it is supposed to bring you luck and have your wish come true," David said.

"No kidding," Nick replied, wondering if he was still hung over.

He watched the crowd, and at the appropriate time, he stepped up, made a wish to get out of Milan alive, and twirled on the testicles.

The foursome walked down to the bend in the drained canal and came upon a street market. There were strange antiques such as old unrecognizable tools, clothes, leather, lots of old junk, music, and interesting people. The street in Milano is like any big city: drugs, mohawks with colors, tattoos, pierced body parts, lots of black jeans, and heavy metal t-shirts. There were lots of anarchists there, and with more than fifty different governments since the end of World War II, Nick would have thought the populous would be tired of anarchy. The constant change of governments had become the status quo.

They stopped for beer on the way back, having taken an extensive walking tour of the city.

The models were still out in force. "Hi Nicholas," a super-esque model type called to him. It was one of Nick's friends from the bathroom search at the *Fiere*.

Nick parted company from his associates and beer to give a hug and do the kiss-kiss thing.

"You remembered my name, Teresa," Nick said.

"And you remembered mine. My brother's name is Nicholas," she said in his ear. "I must go, but I'll see you soon, okay?" Again with the kiss-kiss and off she went.

"Okay," Nick replied in her wake. If he had made a date with her, he surely would have remembered it.

Nick returned to his bewildered associates and finished his beer in silence.

"Nicholas has a way of making friends," Suzanne said.

They made their way back to the apartment and later Suzanne left for a pre-party dinner at *FIG Café*, a restaurant owned by *FIG* agency. Natalie, David, and Nick ate a dinner of pasta.

Natalie and Nick excused themselves to the nearby *Milord Milano* bar and buffet to fortify themselves with margaritas. David and Natalie were still feuding and David elected to stay behind.

Dressed and ready for the next adventure, Natalie and Nick took the tram to the party in their finery. Or at least Nick was. She dressed in a way to get attention, primarily focused on her chest. *I guess if she went to the trouble to have the work done....*

The party was so exclusive that an invitation only got you to the door.

"There is African royalty here tonight, so security is tight," Natalie said, approaching the man with the guest list. She greeted him with a hug and a kiss and they were whisked past the bouncers and into the fray.

After a quick scan of the room, Nick saw Suzanne sitting with Alessandro at a dinner table. The wait staff was removing the evidence of what must have been a fantastic meal. There were a dozen places and as many empty bottles.

Nick felt a tug on his jacket as Skye pulled him into a corner. He felt his heart racing and figured he was grinning like an idiot seeing her again.

"How can I reach you?" she asked with a smile. "I've been thinking of you constantly since we met."

Nick pulled a card from his coat pocket. "I've been thinking about you as well."

"Do you have something to write on?" she asked.

He extracted another card and a fountain pen. She took it and wrote Skye, followed by an email address and telephone number, capped the pen and slid it back into his pocket, affording Nick another whiff of her wonderful scent. She kissed him, this time softly on the lips, put a small package in his hand, and backed away.

"Take care, Nicholas. I will see you again soon," she said and walked backward until the crowd swallowed her. Nick stood there for a moment, watching the last bit of dark hair disappear. *Damn, she was good at that. Why are the women in Milan telling him they will see him soon? Is it an 'until we meet again' sort of thing?*

He slid the package into his pocket and turned around and came face to face with Natalie and Suzanne.

"Come with us. We're off to the dance floor," Natalie said.

"Where did they hide it this time?" he asked, looking around the room.

"I think it's down a flight of stairs, over there," Suzanne pointed. They made their way through the swarm and to the edge of the stairs. There were two large gentlemen in suits—Italy's answer to the sumo wrestler—guarding the first landing of the stairs.

"There's Alessandro," Suzanne called waving. Alessandro leaned forward and spoke to one of the bouncers and pointed to the three of them. Nick walked down the stairs with a beautiful woman on each arm. They were swept past the sentinels of the dance floor and down the remaining steps.

Thirty-Two
I'll take it as a compliment

Nick figured there were no fire marshals in Italy as the basement was packed. They found a seat off to the left of the dance floor, sliding through the crowd.

"Beverages are in order," Nick told his companions.

"Margaritas!" they both cried.

"Of course."

"Here," Natalie said, producing euros from thin air and handing them to him.

"No. I'll get it," Nick said, pulling cash from his pocket. The pickings were slim, only €20. "I didn't realize I was so low on euros."

"Let's see what I have," Suzanne said. They pulled out cash. There were 42 euros when they put it in a pile.

"I'm off," Nick said, propelling himself into the crowd.

"Margaritas!" they both cried again, getting into the spirit of the thing.

It was slow going to the bar; the place was brimming with the international elite of minor princes and baronesses, millionaires, models, and rock stars. Nick nodded hellos along the way, a smile pasted on his face. The place was much better than an airport for people watching.

As Nick approached the bar with their remaining euros, he saw people paying for drinks and taking their receipts to the bar. He slipped sideways to the cash register.

"*Due margaritas,*" he told the woman loudly above the music.

"*Trenta!*" she yelled.

Trenta? Nick thought, not understanding. "*No. Due!*" he yelled back.

"*Trenta!*" she yelled.

"*Oh, trenta.*" It was thirty euros for two margaritas. He dug down, got the bills, paid the woman, and took the receipt to the bar. A moment later, he was wedged in, crammed in from the crowd behind him.

The bartender approached. "*Due margaritas!*" Nick yelled over the music at the bartender, handing him the receipt. There was a lot of yelling going on in Milano discotheques.

"*Due margaritas!*" he yelled back. He shook the beverages, performing the margarita fandango, apparently a specialty in the principality of Milano. Having completed his dance, he poured the drinks into salted glasses. Nick picked up the drinks and attempted to turn around. He realized that he would have the drinks poured down the front of him if he held them at chest level. Nick hoisted them above his head and outboard, and slowly forced himself around, arms held high. The lights went out when he finished his turn, his head wedged between the breasts of a tall black woman. She must have stood 6'7" on her spiked heels. He forced his head back and his chin was firmly caught between soft mounds. He was looking her directly in the mouth. It was full of perfectly even white teeth.

"You look lovely tonight," Nick said.

"Thank you," she replied in an English accent. She gestured with her eyes to the margaritas suspended above us.

"Margaritas for my friends," Nick said.

"Ah, margaritas."

"Margaritas!" yelled the bartender behind them.

"Excuse me one moment," she said.

"*Une margarita,*" she called, sliding her receipt under Nick's arms to the bartender.

"Margarita!" yelled the bartender once more.

"Where are you from?" she asked, lowering her chin so he could see her eyes.

"Honolulu. You are from London?" He could hear the bartender shake the drink behind him.

"Yes," she said, reaching past him and taking her drink from the bar.

"Ready to go?" she asked.

"My right foot first, your left?" Nick asked.

"That should work."

With her margarita behind his back and his hoisted above their heads, they tangoed their way through the crowd. It was slow going. They had plenty of time to get acquainted.

"My name is Angelica," she said.

"Nicholas."

They had to speak loudly to be heard. It was an enforced intimacy, feeling the toned body pressed against his. Nick's view in the stroll was of her smooth neck of creamy chocolate skin, and whatever was in his peripheral vision. What he saw were amused glances in their direction as he walked forward and she backward.

"Where are we going?" Nick asked.

"Just keep going in the direction you are pointing," she said, glancing down.

"Sorry," Nick said.

"I'll take it as a compliment," she said.

"Please do."

Up ahead, the crowd thinned by a person or two, and Angelica turned around. They walked again in unison, this time Nick plastered to her back by the crowd pushing against them. It was an obscene, yet delightful stroll.

"Well, that didn't help. Do you mind if we stand here for a moment, while I, erm, take deep breaths?"

She let out a laugh. "Think of something serious," she said over her shoulder.

"Such as?"

Angelica looked up at the ceiling. "Do you think it's possible for men and women to only be friends?"

"You ask me that, now?"

Angelica threw her head back and laughed again.

"Okay, how about this? What caused you the greatest pain?" she asked.

"Emotional or Physical?"

"Either. Both."

Nick thought for a moment. "Emotional? Losing my parents a few years apart. That was painful."

"Yes, I could see that. How about greatest physical pain?"

"That would be when I was shot," Nick said, wincing at the thought.

"Shot?" Angelica looked at him and cocked her head. "You don't strike me as someone who would get himself shot."

"Until the time it happened, I would have agreed with you."

Angelica stopped by a black man wearing an expensive suit and surrounded by models. Nick and Angelica were able to separate. Angelica said something about royalty. With margaritas still hoisted aloft, Nick bowed to the man. It was more like an extravagant nod than a bow. The man oozed royalty. Nick hoped he wasn't one of Luigi's clients. He gestured to the drinks Nick was holding.

"Margaritas," Nick said by explanation.

"Margaritas," he nodded. The universal language. He smiled and gripped Nick's shoulder.

"I must deliver the goods. My ladies are waiting," Nick said into Angelica's ear.

"Farewell, Nicholas," his statuesque escort said, kissing him on both cheeks.

Nick arrived with the glasses still full, a feat he did not think he'd accomplish.

"Margaritas!" came a hero's welcome from Suzanne and Natalie.

Nick shook his head. *All that for a couple of margaritas. Who would have thought it would be such a life event?*

They shared the drinks, and the three of them headed to the dance floor. There were even more odd people at the party than the one the previous evening. But to Nick, the entire trip had been like dropping into a Star Wars bar. It was a younger crowd and there was evidence of heavy drug use going on. The faces had a spacey far-away look. Nick had heard heroin chic was still the mode in the modeling world.

As they danced, cameras were focused on the three of them. They stayed for another hour and left at 1:30 a.m.

When they got out of the nightclub, a tram was waiting at a stop. Natalie ran up to it and tapped on the glass door.

"*Finito!*" the driver yelled. They had missed the last tram

Natalie, without missing a beat, turned to a well-dressed man sitting in a Mercedes Benz at a stoplight. After a rapid discussion in Italian, the man flicked a switch, and the top folded down. Natalie and Nick tried to pile into the back of his two-seater. They could get into the minuscule back deck, but Suzanne wasn't able to latch her seat in place. Natalie and Nick resembled a pile of laughing formalwear for their efforts and once again Nick found his head buried in breasts. This time firm ones that felt like a pair of old sweat socks.

They extricated themselves and thanked the driver of the Mercedes, who drove off, waving a goodbye salute.

They assessed their financial holdings; it was a mere 12 euros.

"Let's try for a taxi," Natalie said.

"How far can we get for 12 euros?" Nick asked.

"Let's see what we can do," she said.

Natalie quickly flagged down a taxi, then got into a rapid discussion with the driver. Nick was sure having two beautiful foreign women dressed to the nines didn't hurt in the negotiations, and they talked the driver into taking them the entire way home for 12 euros.

"I'm starved," Suzanne said, removing herself from the taxi.

"*Milord Milano*," Natalie and Nick said in unison.

"We have no money," Suzanne said.

"That's okay, we'll do it Italian style. On credit," Natalie replied.

It was a short block to the café where they talked and drank margaritas, and Suzanne perused the buffet. Nick checked the time. It was almost 3:00 a.m. He sat back and surveyed the crowd. The café was a lively place at that hour. Across the room, a woman holding a martini glass danced by herself. Nick removed his jacket and loosened his tie. The woman nodded her approval, did a little twist, and motioned to him to join her. Suzanne and Natalie looked on in surprise when he left the table.

"*Le piacerebbe ballare con me?*" He asked the girl, happy to have finally used the line in Milan.

"You are American?" she asked, swaying to the music.

"*Sono Americano*," Nick replied.

"You dance well," she said.

"Thank you, and so do you."

They danced on to an indistinguishable Eurobeat. The song ended.

"That was nice. But you are exhausted. Please join your friends," she said, kissing him on both cheeks. As soon as she said it, waves of exhaustion flowed over Nick.

She took him by the hand and returned him to his chair and Suzanne and Natalie. She then nodded to them both, turned, and left.

They went back to the apartment and had an odd discussion. It got strange indeed when Natalie said, "I can only go thirty days without sex. On the thirty-first day, I attack someone."

Whatever works, but certainly nothing a man could ever say without repercussions, Nick thought.

It was an appropriate time to end the evening.

Nick did the goodnight kiss thing and left the girls to untangle the web of sex and the sexes. It was 5:30 a.m. when he climbed the stairs to his bed in the loft.

THIRTY-THREE
PIAZZA DEL DUOMO

On Sunday morning, Nick and Suzanne woke around 11:00 a.m., bathed, dressed, and had a quick breakfast of toast and coffee with Natalie and David. Then they walked down to the tram and went onto *Piazza del Duomo* and the geographic center of Milan. There were hundreds of pigeons being fed by locals and tourists alike. They turned to the left and faced the Milan Cathedral or the *Duomo* they had just been to.

Nick had seen plenty of cathedrals in Europe, but the sheer size of the *Duomo* took him by surprise. One of the largest cathedrals in the world, it took nearly six hundred years to complete. Nick stood on the *Piazza*, awestruck, taking it in. The *Duomo* was an imposing force. Nick figured that was by design. But the immense structure didn't feel heavy, despite the mixture of architectural styles including Neoclassic, Baroque, and decorative Gothic. Perhaps it was the 135 spires topped with sculptures of biblical figures, the tallest with a gold Madonna on the tip, reaching more than 350 feet high.

After a few minutes of studying it, he pulled his mobile phone from his pocket and took a photograph, catching a pigeon mid-flight in the frame.

Inside the Cathedral, they stood in the back and listened to the singing during Sunday mass. The ethereal music bounced up and off the walls filling the church. Upon exiting, they stood on the *piazza* and warmed under the blue Italian sky while they watched people pass by.

After that, they trekked to the *Castillo* in the park to view old frescoes and statues, including Michelangelo's last work. Nick thought of it as his "oops". Nick imagined him carving away for days and then hitting a vein in the marble and sending an arm or other appendage crashing to the ground. It must have been a terrible sound. This one appeared to be salvaged from his scrap heap out back. More than likely, it was far from complete. The rough outline of a figure was all that was there. Would Michelangelo even want it displayed? Probably not, thought Nick.

After the intake of culture, they took a walk in the park across from the *Castillo*. There were local street merchants hawking anything from toys to clothes that could rival the designers'.

They caught the tram back to the apartment. Still far from recovering from the previous evening, Nick excused himself for a nap. He awoke to appetizing smells wafting up to the loft. Dinner was a simple and delicious meal of tomato pasta, salad, bread, and wine prepared by Natalie.

Nick did the dishes and was in bed by 10:00 p.m.

THIRTY-FOUR
ONCE MORE UNTO THE BREACH

Monday morning Nick woke up with an uneasy feeling. If he were back on Icarus, he would think there was a storm brewing or he was entering rough water.

He sat up. Suzanne was already downstairs. He reached for his journal and flipped through the pages of the previous week. Luigi's behavior made no sense. Surely, it couldn't all be about Emma Bedford.

He turned to an empty page and documented the events of the previous day.

Then he smelled the coffee and got out of bed.

"Once more unto the breach, dear friends," he said to the empty loft, then descended the stairs to the kitchen and started another day.

When they arrived at *swank* that afternoon, Nick took a whiff. "Luigi is in residence," he said.

"Yes, I can smell that," Suzanne said.

They followed the cologne trail to the conference room and joined Bruce, Valentina, and Luigi at the table. Luigi didn't waste any time on pleasantries. "Why do you think you are here?" he asked Suzanne, slamming his fist on the table.

"I'm here to help you put together the Hawaii operation as you defined it," she replied.

"Help? I don't need your help. When I want help, I buy people and when I'm done, I put them aside," he squeaked. "Are you going to return the money I already gave you?"

It was yet another interesting tactic. Nick tried not to roll his eyes. Here's a guy who told Suzanne he dropped $80,000 in one month of travel in L.A.

"It's not good to make me mad because I get dangerous when I get mad," Luigi said.

Nick was impressed. Suzanne remained calm throughout Luigi's tirade, but he had never been one to take threats lightly.

"You will not threaten Suzanne or me again," Nick said calmly, quietly, looking him directly in the eyes.

Luigi's response gave him away, and for the briefest moment, fear slid across his eyes. He was a bully, only a bully. It was enough for Nick.

"Suzanne, this is all about Emma. Do you wish to continue?" Nick asked her.

She paused and then nodded. "Let's go on."

Whatever glimmer of fear Nick saw in Luigi's eyes faded, and he started ranting again, "Where is Emma?" Nick felt like joining the chorus and pounding on the table along with the beat.

Nick turned to him and talked over him. "Luigi, do you want Emma here?"

Off he went again, "Where is Emma?"

Again, Nick raised his voice above Luigi's. "Do you want a solution to this issue or more and bigger problems?"

He stopped his tirade, a shadow of fear returning to his face.

"If you want Emma, Luigi, this is what it is going to take to get her: housing, a plane ticket, a chaperone and driver, a promotion schedule, and a guarantee for her work," Nick said, mentally ticking off the list.

Luigi was quiet for a moment, leaning back in his chair. "Okay, I agree on the housing and plane tickets, and in principle, of the guarantee. We need to talk about that. I will be her chaperone while she in is Milano."

"How are you going to do that when you are running off to Switzerland for money every two days?" Suzanne asked.

"I can take her to castings." Bruce offered.

Nick looked to Suzanne for confirmation. She nodded. "All right then, what about a promotion schedule?"

Luigi handed Nick a list. He and Suzanne glanced at it. It's like a list of every designer and photographer in Milan.

"That is her schedule," he said.

"I could have copied this out of the phonebook, Luigi. I want dates and times for appointments," Suzanne told him.

"Are you planning to take Emma to any appointments? What do you have planned for her?" Nick asked.

The question set him off again. "Where is Emma?"

"You have all you need to get Emma. You only have to meet the requirements. You have staff in the other room that can make all the arrangements in one hour. All they are doing is reading the newspaper and going outside to smoke cigarettes," Suzanne said.

"Of course, Emma will sign directly with me as her mother agency," Luigi said.

By being Emma's mother agency, he would end residual fees that Suzanne would receive for finding and training Emma. Nick again turned to Suzanne. The man was barking up the wrong piazza. No one in their business would give up a potential top model. He had waited until Monday night to make Suzanne desperate for money.

He miscalculated. His plans for Emma were unclear. He must have known Emma was not coming with them on this trip.

"Luigi, there is no way I will sign over Emma to *swank*. You know it is not done, I know it is not done, everyone in this room knows it is not done. I have too much invested in scouting and training Emma," Suzanne said.

Luigi got up and left the room.

The room remained silent for a while. Nick stared at Bruce across the room, trying to evoke a response. Bruce avoided his gaze and quietly excused himself.

"We are meeting for dinner at *Ristorante Corte Sant Andrea* in thirty minutes," Valentina said, getting up and leaving the room.

Later, back in his office, Luigi blew out a breath.

"Francesca," he called out,

"*Si*?" she answered, coming to the doorway.

Luigi spoke for a while, then opened his desk drawer. He handed Francesca one of Nick's business cards.

"*Si, Luigi*," she said.

"That was something, wasn't it?" Nick said as he and Suzanne walked out to the car.

"Yes, but what?"

"We will probably never know. Are you up for dinner?"

"We have to eat," she said.

"I wonder if Daniel has a couple of really long spoons."

"Hmmm?"

"Supping with the Devil and all that," Nick said.

"Aren't you nervous about this?"

"Of course I am. But much of Luigi is bluster."

THIRTY-FIVE
I THINK WE FELL INTO THE WRONG CROWD

As they arrived at *Ristorante Corte Sant Andrea*, Nick turned to Massimo.

"Massimo, we may retire early this evening."

"Just call me," he said, holding up his cell phone.

"*Grazie.*"

"Good evening, Daniel," Nick said on the way in, handing him their coats. "Thank you for the superb meals. The food and your staff have been excellent."

"We have enjoyed having you here," Daniel said. He reached to the lectern and took a business card, turned it over, and wrote a number on the back. "You are nice people." His eyes shifted toward Luigi talking with Bruce at the bottom of the stairs. "If you have any difficulties, please call me day or night. This is my mobile phone," he tapped his breast pocket and gave Nick a slight smile.

Nick took the card. "Thank you very much. Do you expect we will have difficulties?" Nick asked, bewildered by the growing cadre of supporters they were building in the city.

"One never knows in Milan," Daniel said, taking menus and gesturing toward the stairs.

At the top of the stairs, Nick and Suzanne made a left turn into an alcove filled with a vast table.

"Daniel," Nick said, taking him aside, "Our chauffeur, Massimo, is outside...."

"I will take him to dinner and talk with him."

"Thank you."

"*Prego.*"

Suzanne was seated at the end of the table nearest the door.

Nick joined her. "After Daniel's offer for help, I'd prefer my back to the wall. At least this way we are close to the door."

"What was that about?" she asked.

"I think we fell into the wrong crowd and everyone here knew it but us," Nick replied. "It's neighborly for them to offer their assistance."

Their dinner companions poured in, and three young models, Eli, Enga, and Ginger joined them, all a-twitter about being in Milan.

"Are you girls with *swank*?" Nick asked.

"No, we work for another agency. Luigi invited us to dinner, so we came," Enga said.

"They are so young," Nick said to Suzanne. None of them could have been older than sixteen.

"That's why my models are chaperoned. Sometimes I go with them, sometimes I send parents or grandparents. An underage model never goes alone," Suzanne said.

For Eli and Enga, it was their first trip abroad. They had never been out of the Midwest.

It surprised Nick what made a model. The girls were attractive, pleasant, and easy on the eyes. Nick couldn't bring himself to see them as women. They were your girls' next door—your *very young* girls' next door. They pulled out their cards and tear sheets. Nick found it incredible one person could have so many looks. Their cards were full of juxtapositions. Eli, sitting next to Nick, was a wanton tart in one photo and a polished ingenue in another; a 1980s-era punk rocker, and a beehive-coiffured 1960s leggy thing in yet another. Nick turned to Eli. Without the clothes, makeup, and attitude, she was a young girl out of place in Milan. He then thought of the office in the *swank* agency and the lack of business going on and felt concerned for the girls across the table. Nick took some photos to add to his journal notes. He reached into his jacket pocket and pulled out his mobile phone. "Okay, everyone, model poses." Eli, Enga, and Ginger immediately sprang into action and brought their heads together, and tossed their hair back. Nick shot half a dozen photos of the girls, then turned the camera to the rest of the table and continued shooting, documenting the players.

Nick thought it odd Gabriella was conspicuously absent from the proceedings. And what about Gabriella? She was so far from the business side; it wasn't clear what she did. It was as if her boyfriend gave her the money for the agency, but she was told to let Luigi run it. Her childlike excitement over the *Paris Match* article was telling.

As Nick took the pictures of the dinner party, he couldn't help but wonder, were he and Suzanne relegated to the non-business side of the table? On the other end were Luigi, Bruce, Valentina, a new guy in a dark suit, and a woman with an Irish Setter. It surprised Nick it was acceptable to bring a big dog into a posh restaurant in Italy.

All the people on their side of the table were peripheral to the action. They were out of the way and out of earshot. It was as if Luigi had sat them at the kids' table at Christmas dinner.

Sitting directly across from Nick was a stunning woman named Clara. Clara was Venezuelan and the mistress of the rich, tan, powerful-looking man seated to her left.

Nick knew she was his mistress because that is how he introduced her to him: "This is my mistress, Clara, from Venezuela."

"*Encantada*," Nick said to her.

Clara had perfect features, a perfect figure, and an elegant grace of movement. She flirted with him from across the table. At one point, she took a sip of sparkling wine and winked at Nick in a way that almost made him break his glass.

Nick took out his phone and took a picture of her. She did a fairly playful imitation of the 'model pose' the girls gave him earlier. Her billionaire boyfriend beside her saw the whole thing and was enjoying it as much as she was. He was watching her flirt with Nick and laughing. He looked at Nick and shrugged. It was as if he were saying, "Sure, she can flirt with you all she wants, but she's going home with *me*."

Nick turned to Enga on his left. "Why is Clara trying to kill me with her eye contact?"

"Because she can," Eli and Ginger replied in unison.

Perhaps it was something they learned in Milan.

The salads arrived and across the table, Clara took a languid, sexy bite of greens. Eli, Ginger, and Enga caught the performance. Nick turned to his left as the three young models sat with their mouths gaping open.

"Someone teach me how to do that," Eli said.

"It's something you're born with. It's not possible to teach," Ginger replied most seriously, for she had been out of the Midwest before.

Nick felt a tap on his shoulder and then heard a voice in his ear. It was Daniel.

"Massimo wears a white hat," he whispered to Nick.

"*Grazie*," he replied, amused at the code. He only hoped in Italy it was the good guys who wore the white hats and the bad guys who wore the black ones.

Clara may have had Nick's attention, but he did not neglect the other end of the table: Luigi, the dark suit guy, and Bruce were in conversation throughout the evening. Much of the time, Luigi had his mobile phone to his ear. *Who was he talking to at 10:30 on a Friday evening?*

Dinner came and it was followed by champagne and dessert. They had a rollicking discussion of travel.

"Tell me Nicholas, where is the most exotic place you have visited?" Clara leaned forward and asked. His end of the table stopped talking and waited for his response.

"I'm partial to islands, so I'd have to say Bora Bora in French Polynesia. The color and the temperature of the water are exquisite and the people are friendly. There are little islands called *motus* surrounding the main island. Bora Bora is so beautiful it reaches down into your soul and grabs hold."

"Oh. Ah. *Exotique*" came responses from around the table.

Nick finished his dessert and turned to Suzanne. A tear ran down her cheek.

"What's wrong?"

"I have the worst headache."

"Why don't you freshen up and I'll get Massimo and get us out of here."

"Yes, let's."

She excused herself from the table.

"What's wrong with Suzanne?" Enga asked.

"She doesn't feel well. Too many late nights, I suspect. We will leave soon. It was a pleasure spending the evening with all of you."

The women cooed and made sympathetic noises. "I hope she will be well soon," Clara said.

"I'm sure she will," Nick said. "I need to find Daniel and have him call our driver." He was immediately presented with mobile phones from Enga, Eli, and Clara's boyfriend.

Nick thanked them and pulled his phone from his jacket and dialed Massimo's number.

"*Pronto.*"

"Massimo, it's Nicholas. *Douve es tu?*"

Nick felt a tap on his shoulder. He turned to Massimo standing behind him with his phone in his hand. He had been in the lobby waiting and was fetched by Daniel, who had caught Suzanne on her way to freshen up.

"*Andiamo?*" Massimo asked.

"*Si, andiamo,*" Nick replied.

The week had finally got to Suzanne and the long negotiations were nearly over. They got nowhere. Luigi effectively ended the discussions by walking out of the meeting that afternoon. It was clear what he wanted was not negotiable.

They did damage control early in the week by shopping Emma around to other agencies, so Suzanne had a head start. She also was able to visit the agencies for other work. She could take Emma to *FIG* or *beLLeZZa* or *Salto!*, make her big money, and move on.

Nick reflected on his time in Milan. It had been about Emma. He would be happy not to hear that name again.

They made it back to the apartment and were greeted by Natalie and David. They gave them a blow-by-blow of the meeting with Luigi.

"I think I'll get out of Milan on Wednesday and get to the shows in Paris. I feel threatened by Luigi, and we need to leave," Suzanne said.

Nick had never been one to argue with a woman's intuition, or anyone else's, for that matter.

Thirty-Six

He underestimates you

Tuesday morning Francesca knocked on the doorjamb to Luigi's office. Luigi gestured at the chair across from him. She entered, closed the door, and sat.

She handed him a bound dossier. "This is what I learned about Nicholas Thomas. You will find it very interesting."

For the next hour, Luigi read the documents and made notes.

At the apartment, Nick asked Suzanne, "What's the plan?"

"Luigi texted me this morning. He wants to talk to me alone at 6:30. He specifically asked that you not be in the meeting. He thinks he can sway me if you are not in the room."

"He underestimates you," Nick said.

"Yes, he does. But maybe he's changed and is willing to be reasonable. I'll give him one last chance tonight."

Nick called Massimo to tell him they would go into the office in the afternoon. Suzanne spent the day calling agencies and sending emails, running her business from afar.

Later, they sat in the apartment's salon and compared notes.

"I assume you will be done with Luigi if he hasn't changed his tune?" Nick asked.

"Luigi's not going to steal my models, and he hasn't come through with the money he promised us. So, yes, I suppose I will be done with him."

They ate a late lunch and Nick sat in the bedroom loft, trying to make sense of the trip. He made notes in his journal, outlining the cast of characters. He packed most of his bag for their departure the next day.

With little for him to do, Nick took the time to read more of *The Drifters* until it was time to leave.

George Fairbanks was now in the Spanish city of Pamplona. He arrived during the nine-day *Festival of San Fermín,* which started in the 13th century when bullfights were held to honor the saint. Bulls were let loose in the streets and people would run with them to the bullring. This tradition continued over the years, and in the early 1800s, people started to run with the bulls as sport. The runners, *or mozos,* traditionally wear all white with a red waist sash and red bandana around the neck.

There are surprisingly few injuries during the run, although there are gorings and an occasional death. An average of 2000 people run on weekdays, and 3500 on weekends over the course of the festival.

While in college, Nick and Willie had both read *Death in the Afternoon,* Earnest Hemmingway's treatise on bullfighting, and more on running with the bulls in Hemmingway's *The Sun Also Rises.* While the concept of bullfighting was not appealing to either of them, they had talked about making the journey to Spain to join the run.

Life got in the way, and they never made the trip. Now, an older Nick had no desire to be chased by bulls down a street, or to experience the brutality of a bullfight.

"So I guess this is it," Suzanne said as Massimo pulled up in front of *swank* around 6:15 that evening.

"Yes, I suppose so. If anything is going to happen, now is the time," Nick said.

Once inside, Nick surveyed the scene. "This place is dead, except for that one office down the hall with the young girls coming and going."

"What's that about?" Suzanne asked.

"I don't know. Let's check it out," Nick said.

They walked out the lobby doors and watched a parade of girls go down the hall.

"Those girls do not fit the modeling type. They are attractive enough, but they are not tall enough. I could not get them work," Suzanne said.

They walked down the hall to the line of girls standing outside the door.

"You should probably take the lead," Nick said.

"Hello, girls. Are you part of the *swank* agency?" Suzanne asked.

"Oh, we hope to be," one girl said. "Luigi said we will get paid great, and he places models everywhere in the world."

"Yeah," another girl said, "I get to go to Bah—," she turned to the other girl, "where is that again?"

"Bahrain."

"Yeah, Bahrain. And I'll get paid $60,000 to model there for six months."

"When are you girls leaving?" Nick asked.

"Next week. Luigi said he still needs to make arrangements."

"Has he sent many models on assignment?" Nick asked.

"No. We will be the first group to go. It's really exciting."

They left the girls and went back to the lobby.

"I think Luigi is searching for more than a Grace Kelly for an emir," Nick said. "Did you notice that they had the same look? Blonde, blue eyes, the same body type?"

"Yes, it's like they have been stamped out of a mold. The money Luigi is offering them is too much for a model starting to work. The assignments are too long," Suzanne said.

Nick peered through the window into Luigi's office. Luigi and Bruce were in deep conference, their heads together, poring over documents and talking animatedly.

"Bruce has been spending a lot of time with Luigi lately," Nick said.

"I've noticed."

He took another look at Bruce and Luigi through the window. "I believe Bruce has sold his agency to him."

Nick checked his watch. "It's time for your meeting with Luigi. While you set him straight, I'm going to find an empty office and make a phone call," he said.

He sat at a desk and saw there was a voicemail on his phone. He retrieved the message.

It was Christine Bedford. He listened to the message. "I know this is Nick's number, but Suzanne said her phone didn't work. I need to talk with her before we go on a family vacation. Please call me as soon as possible. I know there is a huge time difference, but it doesn't matter. Just call."

Should he wait for Suzanne? She was in with Luigi, and that could take hours. Christine Bedford made a return call sound urgent.

The twelve-hour time difference would make it 6:30 a.m. in Hawaii. At least it's not earlier, Nick thought, calling her back.

"Thank you for calling," Christine said. "Emma and I wanted to talk to you before we leave tomorrow night."

"So tell me, where are you going on your vacation?" Nick asked.

"Oh, we are just going to take the family away for a week. Nothing special."

"The outer islands?"

"No, just a vacation." Nick heard a cough in the background.

"So, Nick. Tell us about Milan," Emma asked.

Nick started in on his tale. He directed his comments to Emma. Since it was her life that was being manipulated.

Should he tell them it was possible Emma would be sold into white slavery or some form of prostitution? He had no proof of that.

"I think *swank* is a front for something odd. I have no idea what it is they do. They are not an active modeling agency. I am not sure where you will end up if you take a job."

"I want her working soon. Suzanne should have something for her by now," Christine Bedford said.

Nick ignored the mother. "Emma, there are much better agencies than *swank*, big agencies with big-name models. *swank* is at the bottom of the list. I don't think it's *on* the list. Listen carefully, Emma. Luigi is not a nice person. We asked around, and no one had a single good word about the agency. Suzanne will go to Paris tomorrow to find the best place for you."

"That sounds good," Emma said.

"But Luigi has promised us a lot of money upfront," Christine Bedford said.

"You have talked to Luigi directly?"

"He called us early this morning."

Was that who Luigi was talking to on his mobile phone at dinner the previous evening?

"Luigi agreed to pay Suzanne to come to Milan to explore starting a business with him. He still owes her half of what he promised to pay her when we arrived."

Nick could hear Christine and Emma talking in low voices. The conversation turned into a hissing argument. He could make out the words 'money' and 'first class'. Nick waited until they were done.

"So Emma, are you looking forward to your vacation?"

"Oh, we'll only be away for a couple of weeks," her mother answered for her.

It was obvious to Nick they were going to Milan. *Did Christine not care about her daughter's well-being? Was the money that important to her to want to sell out her child?*

Luigi had done an end run. That was clear enough. Emma's mother was teaching Emma how to lie.

"We need to go. We need to pack for our trip," Christine Bedford said.

Before they ended the call, Nick felt the need to say one more thing.

"Emma," Nick said

"Yes?"

"Please be very careful on your family vacation."

"Goodbye, Nick," Christine Bedford said, ending the call.

Nick pulled out his journal and made notes of the phone call. He was frustrated and angry with Christine Bedford and appalled at her lack of concern for her daughter.

He finished his note-taking and pulled Maddie's card from his wallet and dialed her number. "Hello, Maddie. This is Nicholas Thomas. We met in the coffee line at the shows and again at the *FIG* party."

"Of course, Nicholas. How are you?"

"I'm perplexed, and I hope you can shed some light. Do you have time to talk now?"

"Yes, this is a good time."

"What do you know of Luigi Donati?"

After a few seconds of dead air, Nick asked, "Are you still there?"

"Are you, erm, working with Mr. Donati?"

"I wouldn't say working with him. He is trying to take advantage of my client, and one of her models." Nick thought back to his brief interaction with Maddie. "May I speak confidentially?"

"Yes, that would be best for both of us."

"I have concerns regarding Mr. Donati," Nick told her of his observation of the lack of traffic in the building, the promises broken to Suzanne, the photos of her models on the walls, and the young girls in the office awaiting long-term modeling jobs in other countries at unheard of rates, and his focused desire to have Emma Bedford come to Milan.

"I can understand your concerns," Maddie said. "Mr. Donati is a newcomer to the business. He has used aggressive—some might even consider them strong-arm tactics trying to get into the business. He is quickly developing a reputation. People are speaking in hushed tones about his associates."

"What are people saying about his associates?"

"I shouldn't be talking with you about this. I don't even know you," Maddie said.

"I assure you, whatever you tell me will not be traced back to you."

There was another pause on the call. "You seem like a good person. I guess I will trust you."

"And his associates?"

"There are rumblings he is connected to organized crime, but no one will come out and say it."

"Organized crime? Terrific."

"You should be careful. I need to go. We should probably not talk again." Maddie said. She spoke quickly, with fear in her voice.

"I understand. Thank you for your time. Again, I assure you, what you told me will not be attributed to you."

THIRTY-SEVEN
I'VE SEEN ENOUGH

Back in Luigi's office, Suzanne sat across from him and waited to hear why she was summoned.

"How well do you know this man, Nicholas Thomas?"

Suzanne squirmed in her seat. *What is this?* "He was recommended to me in Honolulu. I haven't known him that long," she said.

"I do not think he is the man you think he is. Please read the marked passages in this dossier."

Luigi passed a bound document across his desk.

Suzanne opened the cover and flipped through the pages and came to a marked section. It was an article from a San Francisco newspaper dated a few years ago.

Local Entrepreneur Under FBI Investigation
in Embezzlement Scheme

Local businessman Nicholas Thomas, a San Francisco native, is being investigated by the FBI regarding his role in the embezzlement of $32 million from investors in his company. The funds disappeared along with Mr. Thomas' partner, Lance Grabowski.

Nicholas Thomas is the son of the deceased prominent local attorney Peter Thomas of Thomas Law, LLC. Thomas Law was a boutique law firm representing many prominent San Francisco families, including one who sued this newspaper for libel. Nicholas Thomas and John Mitchell, the FBI Special Agent in charge of the investigation, were not available for comment.

Suzanne continued to skim the dossier. Much of the information was the same, but from different sources.

It all looked bad.

"So what happened to Nick?"

"He's probably still under investigation," Luigi lied. Later articles, which he had Francesca omit from the dossier, stated that there was no evidence Nick Thomas had any involvement in the crime. But that didn't help Luigi's case, and he wanted to drive a wedge between Suzanne and Nick Thomas and get him out of the picture.

Suzanne sat back in her chair.

"You can keep the dossier if you wish," Luigi said.

"No, thank you. I've seen enough."

THIRTY-EIGHT

I'm almost afraid to ask

After Nick ended the call, he sat quietly and considered his options. Luigi had become more adamant and angry with the passing days. He had dropped the pretext of a joint partnership with Suzanne and her agency and was only focused on his goal of getting Emma to Milan. He was a man obsessed.

Maddie's comments put things in a different light.

With the new information from Maddie, and what Suzanne and Nick learned from talking with young girls in the office at the end of the hall, Nick felt the need to do something, even if it was only based on supposition. According to the girls he and Suzanne talked to, Luigi had sent none on an assignment, so there was still a chance to stop it before it started, to protect Emma Bedford from whatever fate was in store for her.

Whatever "it" was.

It couldn't be good.

He looked out the window to the darkening sky. Lights were coming on around the city.

He picked up his mobile phone once again. It was approaching 10 a.m. in San Francisco.

"I'm almost afraid to ask." Special Agent John Mitchell answered Nick's call on the first ring.

"How do you know this isn't a social call?" Nick asked.

"Is it?"

"No."

"What have you gotten yourself into now?"

"Human trafficking?" Nick said.

Despite the enthusiastic reporting by San Francisco newspapers, Nick Thomas was indeed no longer a suspect in the loss of his fortune, and John Mitchell and Nick Thomas had become friends of sorts. At least they had mutual respect for one another. They had even saved each other's lives.

"Jeeze, Nick. Human trafficking?"

"It looks like it."

"This is going on in Honolulu?"

"No, I'm in Italy. Milan." Nick filled Mitchell in on what he suspected was going on at the *swank* offices.

Mitchell had Nick start at the beginning, asking questions and wanting as much detail as Nick could give. Nick outlined the players: Suzanne, Luigi, and the others. Nick knew the first names of some of the girls, but not their last. They discussed the star of the show, Emma Bedford. Nick could tell Mitchell had put him on speakerphone and was taking notes in full-blown interrogation mode.

"I kept a journal and took pictures of some of the players," Nick said.

"Of course you did. You are always thorough. Please send them to me."

"I will." Nick checked his watch. Suzanne had been with Luigi for more than an hour. "I need to check in on Suzanne. She's been in a meeting with Luigi. A meeting he excluded me from."

"Keep your phone close. I need to run this through the FBI Interpol liaison."

"One more thing. Can you get in touch with Emma Bedford and her mother? They need to be told what is going on. They wouldn't listen to me."

"I'm on it. I've got to go now. Be careful, Nick."

THIRTY-NINE
HE'S UP TO SOMETHING

After Suzanne left Luigi's office, he sat back in his chair and closed his eyes for a minute. He then leaned forward, opened his eyes, picked up the phone, and made a call.

He took the dossier and left the building.

At a café a few blocks away, Luigi met with a tall, muscular man wearing a tailor-made suit. His hair was short and in a military cut, his eyes intense and piercing.

"What about the woman?" the man asked.

"Leave her alone, Marco. All she wants is the money I lured her here with. But keep an eye on her. Have your team follow her."

"And the man?"

"I'll text you the photo I took of him last night. He's up to something. He's been talking to the girls. Blackmail? I don't want to wait to find out. It's time for Nicholas Thomas to learn who he's dealing with."

FORTY

DID SHE SAY WHERE SHE WAS GOING?

After his discussion with Mitchell, Nick walked to Luigi's office to find Suzanne. "Luigi left for the day," Francesca said.

"Where's Suzanne?"

"Suzanne also left," Francesca said.

"Did she say where she was going?"

"No. When I went into Luigi's office, they were both gone."

The sun had fully set by the time Nick walked out of the lobby and to the street to Massimo, who was parked at the curb, talking on the phone. He hung up when Nick got into the car.

"Where's Suzanne?" Nick asked.

"She got into a taxi and left about an hour ago."

"Did she say where she was going?"

"No, she walked right past the car and didn't say anything. She was in a hurry."

"I'll call her," Nick said, pulling his phone from his pocket.

He let the phone ring until it went to voice mail. He left her a message to call him.

"That's odd."

"Maybe her battery died," Massimo said.

"I'll try again." Once again, the call went to voice mail.

"Maybe she headed back to the apartment."

"Perhaps." He was at a loss. "I'll call Natalie."

He dialed her number.

"Natalie, it's Nick. I haven't been able to reach Suzanne. Is she at the apartment?"

"No, she came by, picked up her bag, and left directly for the airport."

What had Luigi said to her?

"So, heading to Paris?"

"I suppose," Natalie said.

"Is she okay?" he asked.

"She seemed fine. Why?"

Nick saw no reason to get Natalie involved. "Just crossed signals, I guess."

"She said you were booked on a flight out in the morning."

"Where to?" Massimo asked.

"Give me a moment to sort things out," Nick said. His head was swimming. The mess was beyond damage control. Suzanne had decamped in a hurry, probably because of whatever Luigi said to her.

Nick knew it was also his time to leave.

"Let's go to the apartment and get my suitcase. I'll find another place to stay tonight."

"Okay," Massimo said, starting the car.

When they arrived at the apartment, Nick asked Massimo to wait while he retrieved his bag.

When he entered the apartment, Natalie was in the kitchen.

"Hey, Nick. Luigi called right after you did."

"Did he say what he wanted?"

"He wanted to talk to Suzanne. When I told him she had left for the airport, he asked for you. He seemed angry."

"I came by to get my suitcase," he said, heading upstairs to the loft.

"I'm going to catch an early flight. Thank you for your hospitality," Nick said.

"No problem. It was nice having you here. You and Suzanne should coordinate better, though."

"We really should," he agreed.

FORTY-ONE
SUZANNE STARED BLANKLY OUT THE WINDOW

In the taxi on the way to the airport, Suzanne reflected on the trip. First, Luigi turned out to be a hothead with violent tendencies who ran across the border to Switzerland for cash. He was unknown in the industry and trying to jumpstart an agency by stealing hers. Bruce and Valentina were in bed with Luigi. Then there was the question of the girls in the back office to whom Luigi made outrageous financial promises. That smacked of something terrible. She would have to think hard and make discrete inquiries before taking it further. She could do that from Paris. Protecting young models was the reason Suzanne stayed in the business. There had always been predators in the fashion industry, male and female, straight and gay. She felt a responsibility to her models and their parents. Christine Bedford was an outlier. Suzanne had never had a parent so cavalier regarding their daughter's well-being.

Then there is Nick Thomas. He obviously has a checkered past. She had seen it too often in the business. Scammers and wannabes—there was always someone on the grift. It was the norm for the industry.

So she took *French leave* and got out of town, telling no one but Natalie. She owed her that much.

The fashion shows were moving to Paris next, and she would continue her business there.

Suzanne stared blankly out the window.

Nick sure had her fooled for a while. He genuinely gave the impression of being a good guy.

Didn't they all?

Forty-Two
There's a Chinatown in Milan?

Back at the car, Massimo was waiting with the trunk open. Nick put in his suitcase and they got back in the car.

"Where to now?"

"Do you know a hotel where I can stay the night?"

"I have a friend who works at the *Hotel Viu* near Chinatown. I'm sure he can get you a room there," Massimo said.

"There's a Chinatown in Milan?"

"There is."

"*Hotel Viu* it is."

They were driving down *Viale Tunisia* when Massimo received a call. He pushed a button on the steering wheel and answered. Nick watched him listening intently.

"*Si, si. Sei sicuro?*" Massimo asked.

Massimo turned down a side street and checked his mirror again.

"Okay," he said, "*Millie grazie.*" He took his mobile phone from his pocket, lowered the window, threw it across the intersection, and accelerated.

"My friend has connections in the, let's say, not-so-good side of Milano," Massimo said, raising the window. He turned down another side street. "Certain people are looking for an American named Nicholas Thomas. They are told to find him and detain him—with force, if necessary."

"That white Lancia, is it still behind us?" Massimo asked, making a sharp turn. He reached into the glove box and extracted another mobile phone. He pushed buttons and synced the Bluetooth to the car, then slid the phone into his breast pocket. "I always carry a spare," Massimo said.

Nick turned and looked out the back window. The car behind them sped up and made the same turn.

"Yes, they're still there."

FORTY-THREE

They were traveling at high speed through the back streets of Milan. Massimo's eyes darted back and forth, his hands loose on the steering wheel, his movements sure and smooth.

Nick's brain went into overdrive. Mitchell was too far away to be of much help.

He pulled out his phone and dialed.

"Good evening, Horatio. It's Nick Thomas."

"Nick, I didn't expect to hear from you. How have you been?"

"I need an extraction."

"Send me your coordinates now," Horatio said.

Nick used his mobile phone to share his location with him.

"You are in the Navigli District in Milan," Horatio said.

"I suppose that's where I am. We are moving at quite a clip."

"Stand by one moment." There was a pause and Nick braced himself as Massimo made a sliding turn. Horatio came back on the line.

"What's going on, Nick?"

"I may have stumbled on the trafficking of young girls in Milan. My driver got word I was to be detained by force and now we are being chased by a white Lancia. I've already reached out to a contact at the FBI, and he is getting in contact with Interpol."

"John Mitchell?"

"How do you know it was John Mitchell I called?"

"I like to know who I am dealing with," Horatio said. "I did a background check when we met and learned of your troubles in San Francisco. I talked to a friend at the FBI. He put me on to John Mitchell. We had a long talk. Mitchell speaks highly of you."

"I guess I should have expected you would check up on me. By the way, my client may be in trouble. She was headed to Paris. But now I'm not sure she wasn't abducted."

Nick told him how she left unexpectedly and then gave Horatio Suzanne's full name and contact information, including email and telephone number.

"I'll get on to my contacts at the airlines to find out if she has a flight out. She was going out of Malpensa?"

"I assume so. It was only a few hours ago that she left Luigi's office."

"I'll get someone on her wherever she is and make sure she is safe."

"Thank you. I'm concerned about her."

"You need to get out of Italy. Can you make it across the border to Switzerland? It is only an hour or an hour and a half by car to Lugano."

"Hold on a moment." Nick turned to Massimo. "Massimo, I need to get to Lugano. Do you have a car I can use? They will be looking for you and this car. I've already put you in enough danger."

"One moment, Nicholas," Massimo pushed a button on the steering wheel and spoke.

"*Chiama, Allegra.*"

There was the ringing of the phone and then an answer.

"*Pronto,*" a voice said.

Massimo fired off a torrent of rapid Italian. Allegra responded with a salvo of her own. A moment later Massimo disconnected the call.

"I have someone who will drive you there. You can leave right away," Massimo said.

Nick spoke back into the phone, "Yes, I can get to Lugano."

"I heard. Good. Make your way to the *Hotel Gabbani* on the *Piazza Cioccaro*. They will take good care of you."

"*Hotel Gabbani* on *Piazza Cioccaro*. Got it."

Massimo made another sliding turn onto a side street.

"When we end this call, you need to lose your cell phone. If I can track you, someone else can, too. The same for your driver."

"Massimo has already thrown one phone out the window and is talking on another one."

"Then you are in good hands, but it would be helpful to have a way to communicate."

"Just a second," Nick leaned forward, "Massimo, I need a phone."

Massimo handed his phone over the seat to Nick. "I can get another later."

"Horatio, Massimo gave me his spare," Nick said, reading the number to him off the back of the phone.

"I'll get on to contacts I have in law enforcement in Italy that I can trust and light a fire under them."

"I can't thank you enough, Horatio."

"Lose the Lancia."

"Massimo's working on it."

"I will be in touch," Horatio said, ending the call.

FORTY-FOUR
SIT BACK AND HOLD ON

"Sit back and hold on," Massimo said. The Alfa Romeo shot forward as he accelerated.

Nick rolled down his window and tossed his mobile phone into a canal, then looked out the back window. "You're losing them."

Nick kept his eye on the following car. After a few more turns, he had lost sight of it. Massimo made a controlled sliding turn into an alleyway. He turned off the headlights, and they shot through the narrow dark passage. He made another turn and turned the headlights back on. They drove on for ten more minutes, making turns down other alleys and side streets.

Finally, Massimo drove into a courtyard and came to a stop. A full-sized BMW sedan sat idling off to the side. A woman dressed entirely in black stood beside the open trunk.

Nick and Massimo got out of the car. Nick retrieved his suitcase as Massimo talked to the driver.

When Nick approached, Massimo introduced them. "Nicholas, this is my cousin, Allegra. She will drive you to Lugano."

"*Ciao, Allegra,*" Nick said, shaking her hand.

"Nice to meet you, Nicholas," she said in perfect English. She took Nick's suitcase and put it in the trunk, and pulled on black driving gloves. "Now we should leave."

Nick turned to Massimo. "I can't thank you enough, Massimo."

"You are welcome. I enjoyed driving you. I rarely get to drive my car like that. Please give my regards to Suzanne when you talk to her."

"I will. At least let me buy you a couple of mobile phones."

Massimo put his hand on Nick's shoulder. "I was due for an upgrade. Now go."

Nick climbed into the front seat, and Allegra sped off.

FORTY-FIVE
ARE YOU SURE THAT'S HIM?

"What do you mean you lost them?"

Luigi was sitting in his apartment, looking out at the city lights.

Marco squirmed in the seat of his car. "We tracked the driver's phone and one of our men spotted Nick Thomas. When he gave chase, his driver lost him," Marco said.

"Massimo," Luigi said, shaking his head. "I never should have brought in an outsider. Where are they now?"

"They were in Navigli heading north. They could be anywhere now," Marco said.

"And in any car," Luigi added.

"I have our people watching all the entrances to the autostradas. They have a photo of Nick Thomas with them. I also have men at the airport and train stations."

"Anyone following us?" Allegra asked.

"Not that I can tell," Nick replied.

"Me, either."

Nick's phone rang and he answered with the speakerphone on. "What car are you in and what is your location and what is your speed?" Horatio asked.

"Hold on." Nick held the phone up to Allegra.

"Black BMW 8-Series. We are about to join the A8. We are going the maximum legal speed of one-hundred and thirty kph," she said, glancing at the speedometer. She also told Horatio the number plate of the BMW.

"I have arranged an escort to Lugano for you. I have a team nearby returning to Gstaad from a job in Genoa. Two cars, both Mercedes, are racing to catch up with you. When they do, keep pace with the lead car."

"Okay," Allegra said.

"I'll get back to you." Horatio ended the call.

Allegra drove past two men sitting in an idling Maserati sedan near the entrance of the A8.

"That looks like Thomas," one of the men said, taking a glance at the photo on his mobile phone.

"Are you sure?" the driver pulled onto the autostrada behind the BMW.

"It looks like him. I'll tell Marco we may have spotted him and for him to have someone man our position in case I'm wrong."

"Marco told everybody to follow at a distance and see where they are headed."

Allegra and Nick continued on the A8, the *Autostrada dei Laghi* —the *Motorway of the Lakes* to the A9, driving north to the nearest Swiss border at Chiasso. They were both deep in thought as they continued on their journey.

The men in the Maserati were keeping their distance in a different lane, with a couple of cars between them and the BMW.

"Are you sure that's him?" the driver asked.

"I said it looks like him. We would be in big trouble if it was and we didn't follow him."

"Yes, I suppose so."

Two black Mercedes sedans, each carrying two men, shot past the Maserati and took up position beside the BMW.

"Are they ours?" the driver of the Maserati asked.

"I don't recognize them."

The first Mercedes pulled up beside the BMW and Allegra gestured to the driver to take the lead. He sped up and got in front of them while the second car took the position behind. The lead car gradually increased speed until the three cars were cruising at 180 kilometers per hour.

"This is great," Allegra said with a grin on her face and her eyes on the road.

"Who is your friend Horatio? He must be very well connected."

"He has a private security company," Nick said.

"What is his company called?"

"*Cerberus.*"

"*Cerberus*? That company has an exclusive and wealthy clientele. You must be an important client of Horatio's."

"He's just a friend," Nick said.

"Nice friend to have."

FORTY-SIX
A SKILLFULLY EXECUTED MANEUVER

A few minutes later, Horatio called Nick. "I hear your escort has arrived."

"Yes, they're here," Nick replied.

"I have John Mitchell of the FBI on the line, Commander Rebecca Rossetti of the Lugano Canton Police in Switzerland, and Claudio Russo, Deputy Director of the *Direzione Investigativa Antimafia* in Italy. The DIA is the Anti-Mafia Investigation Directorate that has been investigating Luigi Donati."

"Hello," Nick replied.

"Hello, Nick. Horatio informs me you are on your way to Switzerland," John Mitchell said.

"Yes. Thank you for coordinating with him."

Horatio cleared his throat. "Both the Swiss and Italian Agencies are in their offices with their staff on speakerphones. They have questions for you."

The heavy luxury car made for a quiet ride, even at speed. While Allegra kept pace with the other cars toward the Swiss border, Nick fielded questions. The Italians focused on human trafficking, the Swiss dealt with the financial aspects of the case.

Nick found it interesting both of them were differential to Horatio. He checked his watch. In less than an hour, Horatio had assembled powerful groups from two nations—and after working hours.

Back in the Maserati, the driver looked at his speedometer. "The BMW has a protection detail and they've increased speed."

"I see that. I think they are heading to Switzerland."

"It looks that way."

The man in the right seat dialed his phone and spoke for a while.

"*Si, Marco. Capisco.*" He ended the call, reached behind his seat, and retrieved a rifle.

"We are to stop them before they get to the Swiss border," he said, lowering the window and resting the rifle on the door. "Ready?"

"Ready." The driver put his foot to the floor and closed the gap with the trailing Mercedes.

Allegra broke in on the conversation with the Swiss and Italian authorities and Nick. "Something is going on behind us."

Nick looked back to see the trailing car swerving across the lanes behind him and a set of headlights behind the Mercedes.

"He's blocking a car," Nick said. "That's not good."

"Horatio, we have company. Luigi's men must have found us." Nick said into the phone. Then he saw flashing dots of light from behind the trailing car and heard the report of gunshots. "They're shooting at our rear escort."

In a skillfully executed maneuver, the lead Mercedes pulled into the right lane and slowed, allowing Allegra to pass.

"My team will block the following car. Their cars are armored. Tell your driver to go all out for the Swiss border," Horatio said.

Nick turned back to Allegra. Her eyes were wide and shifted between the action in the rearview mirror and the road ahead. "Okay, Allegra. Let's see what your car can do. Get us to Switzerland."

"Yes, I believe that is a good idea," she said, flipping switches on the dashboard. Driving lights lit up the road nearly a kilometer ahead. She took a last look in the rearview mirror. "I've been wanting to do this." She pushed down the gas pedal and the V8 engine with twin turbochargers immediately responded.

Nick felt like he had been shot out of a cannon.

"Oh wow," Nick said, tightening his grip on the door handle. He looked back as the lights of the cars faded in the distance. The speedometer was touching 290 kilometers per hour.

"This car was very fast before I had it modified. I still have room in the pedal," Allegra said, her eyes focused on the road ahead.

Nick looked out the window at Italy flashing by. "This is probably fast enough."

"Yes, I don't want to overrun my headlights."

Back on the phone, Nick said, "We're on our own, now, Horatio."

"They are expecting you at the border," Rebecca Rossetti said.

"Stay on the line, Nick. We will coordinate from here while you continue to Lugano," Horatio said, followed by a cascade of discussion in the background.

At the speed they were driving, the distance to Switzerland evaporated. Soon they could see flashing lights in the distance.

There were Swiss and Italian police cars lining the road at the border.

Allegra slowed and came to a stop as armed guards moved behind the BMW, looking out to Italy.

"Do you have your passport?" Allegra asked.

"I have it right here," Nick said, taking it out of his breast pocket.

A guard approached the car and Allegra handed him their passports.

He opened them, took a glance, and leaned into the car.

"Nicholas Thomas?" he asked.

"Yes?"

"Welcome to Switzerland," he said, throwing a salute to him.

"Thank you."

"Wow, I suspect you were being modest before. You must be a powerful person," Allegra said.

"Someone is," Nick said, sitting back in his seat. He could feel his heartbeat returning to normal.

In rapid Italian, Allegra told the guard they were being chased and their two Mercedes escort cars were behind them acting as shields to gunfire.

"Yes, we have been in contact with the Commander of the Lugano Canton Police."

A few minutes later, the two Mercedes with Horatio's men pulled in behind them.

The guard leaned in the window. "Your security detail was successful in blocking the cars, and your pursuers turned off on the last exit before the border and stayed in Italy. The Italian police are in pursuit with both ground and air units."

That was followed by a flurry of shuffling cars as Nick's escort grew in number. A white BMW with orange stripes with POLIZEI on it took the lead in front of the first Mercedes and another POLIZEI had taken up behind the trailing Mercedes, with Nick and Allegra in the BMW in the middle. Nick could see the damage to the back of the Mercedes in front of him. The window was pitted and there were dents in the trunk and rear of the car. Both taillights were missing—shot out from the gunfire.

FORTY-SEVEN

Nick spoke into his phone. "Okay, Horatio, we can continue now."

The conversation with the Italian and Swiss law enforcement teams continued as they drove to Lugano.

This time, the cars were going closer to the speed limit, with the front and rear police cars running with flashing lights.

A group of people in dark suits were standing at the curb when the five cars pulled in front of the alley to *Hotel Gabbani*. Nick and Allegra got out of their car, followed by four Swiss police officers, and the four men in Horatio's escort cars.

One of the crowd approached Nick. "I am Rebecca Rossetti, Commander of the Lugano Cantonial Police." She showed him her identification.

"Nicholas Thomas. It is a pleasure to meet you in person."

They shook hands.

Rebecca Rossetti turned to the two uniformed police officers. "*Grazie, signori.*" The officers saluted and took up guard in front of the hotel.

Nick saw Allegra in an animated discussion with the driver of the following Mercedes. The driver was gesturing to Allegra's BMW.

The driver of the lead Mercedes approached Rebecca Rossetti. "We have been instructed to maintain a perimeter around the building, and Mr. Thomas," he said.

"That is fine. We have the use of the fourth-floor rooftop bar of the *Ikobani Restaurant*. We can be secure and private there." She gestured toward the lobby door.

"One moment, please," Nick said, turning and walking to Allegra. Horatio's men followed.

"Thank you, Allegra. You drive brilliantly."

Allegra handed Nick his suitcase.

"I've never had so much fun—and excitement."

"If you give me your contact information, I will be sure to send you something for your trouble," Nick said.

"My boyfriend lives in Porlezza on Lake Lugano, about 20 kilometers from here. I will stay with him for a couple of days. So, no, I won't take your money."

"Thank you, again."

They shook hands, and Nick followed Rebecca Rossetti into the lobby. An officer approached Nick and took his luggage from him.

"My associate will have you checked in to your suite. When you freshen up, he will take you upstairs, where we can continue our discussion," Rebecca Rossetti said.

"I'm sure I can find my way," Nick said.

"I have been directed that you are protected until the matter of Luigi Donati has been resolved. There have already been two car chases earlier this evening."

"An escort will be fine," Nick said

Rebecca Rossetti didn't know what to make of the call from the Swiss Office of the Attorney General directing her to work with Horatio Martín to expedite the investigation of Luigi

Donati. Then there was the American Nicholas Thomas and his connection to the FBI in San Francisco. Horatio Martín had spoken of Mr. Thomas in high regard, but Thomas wasn't part of the FBI.

Ten minutes later, Nick had shaved and brushed his teeth and been escorted to the rooftop bar to join Rebecca Rossetti.

"You said you have kept a journal of your time in Milan?" she asked.

"Yes." Nick took his journal out of his laptop case and opened it.

"Let me get my Italian counterparts on the phone and you can share the details with all of us. That will speed the process."

Nick read through his journal day by day. Rebecca Rossetti and the Italians asked for clarification on points and the spelling of names. He showed her pictures of the players he had taken on his mobile phone.

"Please send the photos to me and I will forward them to my colleagues. You have much useful information here," she said.

"It's more detailed later when I realized there was something strange going on."

"Tell me about Valentina Moretti and Bruce Caputo."

"I honestly think they are desperate idiots. Perhaps you will discover more. I suspect they both sold their agencies to Luigi, but I have no proof."

The questions went on for hours. Nick checked his phone. It was 1:34 in the morning.

"I have a question for you," Nick said.

"I will answer it if I am able," Rebecca Rossetti replied.

"I'm no legal expert. But what evidence do you have to go after Luigi Donati? It seems he is about to break some laws. How do you stop him before a girl or girls disappear?"

"That is an astute question. The answer is Luigi Donati has been under investigation for money laundering, wire fraud, conspiracy, and bank fraud. The Italian Government has had for some time enough evidence to charge Signore Donati on multiple counts of each crime. They have avoided arresting him to gather the names and identities of other players in his organization."

"With innocent people at risk, they no longer have the luxury of waiting?" Nick asked.

"That is correct. They may not have the identities of every party involved, but Donati and his associates will be much older when they are released from incarceration."

FORTY-EIGHT
LUGANO

The next morning, Nick and Horatio were sitting in the deserted rooftop bar of the *Ikobani Restaurant* at the *Hotel Gabbani.*

Nick was eating a breakfast of oatmeal with fresh fruit, Horatio an omelette. They both had cups of espresso in front of them.

"How did you get here so fast?" Nick asked.

"I was in Gstaad with a client and I had a few days off while he was with his family. It was a four-hour drive and I got in at about two-thirty this morning." He slid a cell phone across the table. "You can use this. It's set up for international calls. I put John Mitchell's number in the phone. Please give him my regards."

"Thanks." Nick picked up the phone.

"Rebecca Rossetti will be back here within the hour," Horatio said. "You will be busy, so enjoy your meal while you can."

A short time later, Rebecca Rossetti joined them in the rooftop bar. "You must be Horatio Martín," she said.

"Commander Rossetti, I presume," Horatio said, standing and shaking her hand.

"You and Mr. Thomas have certainly stirred up this part of Europe."

"That was Luigi Donati's doing," Horatio said.

"Yes, you are correct about that." She turned to Nick. "We have more to talk about this morning."

"I'm going to leave you to it and take a nap. I need more than three hours of sleep," Horatio said, excusing himself.

After he left, Rebecca Rossetti said, "You are very well connected."

"It would seem so. Where does the investigation stand?"

"Human trafficking is a foremost priority for the EU. The modeling industry in Milan has been long associated with predatory men seeking young women. There is a similar problem in Paris. The Jeffrey Epstein affair in the United States has punctuated the need for greater vigilance in these matters."

"I can imagine," Nick said.

Rebecca Rossetti glanced at her notes. "The *Carabinieri* in Milano surrounded the home of Luigi Donati at six this morning. He and his associates in Milan have been arrested."

"That's a good start," Nick said.

"The girl Emma Bedford and her mother were visited by the FBI in Honolulu. The daughter admitted to the agent they were traveling to Milan to meet with Luigi Donati. FBI Special Agent Leland Chan strongly suggested they cancel their trip. They took Agent Chan's advice and are staying home. He is taking their statement now."

"That's good to hear. I was sure they were going to Milan. I never bought the family vacation angle," Nick said.

"Special Agent Chan sends his regards to you," Agent Rossetti said with a quizzical look. Nick had met Chan in Honolulu when he and John Mitchell had teamed up when Nick once again found himself in the wrong place at the wrong time.

"And my client, Suzanne Langston? Is she safe?"

"Ms. Langston was met coming off the plane at Charles de Gaulle by a team from *The Cerberus Group*. She was being followed by one of Mr. Donati's associates, who was detained by *Cerberus* and turned over to the authorities in Paris."

"Horatio said he would send someone to make sure she was safe." Nick was no longer surprised at Horatio's reach.

"Ms. Langston has been debriefed by authorities in Paris and given a protection detail until we ascertain Mr. Donati's organization and anyone associated with it has been immobilized."

"And the girls at the *swank* agency?" Nick asked.

"Mr. Donati moved up their departure dates to tomorrow. Thanks to you, and with the names and pictures you gave us, we got to them in time. We were able to get them all to safety. As far as we can tell, no girls have been sent on assignment."

"More good news."

"The arrests have been made by the *Carabinieri* in Italy and *Police Nationale* in France, what used to be called the *Sûreté*," Rebecca Rossetti said.

"It must have been a busy night," Nick said.

"Indeed. Now that you are caught up, I would like to ask you questions to fill in the gaps," Agent Rossetti said.

"Of course," said Nick. "But I need coffee. May I get you a cup?" Nick asked, moving to the coffee pot at the bar. The hotel manager had kept a fresh pot available throughout the proceedings.

"Yes, please. Like your friend, Mr. Martín, I need more than three hours of sleep. The coffee will help."

When Nick finished his interview with Rebecca Rossetti, he returned to his room and slept until 5:00 p.m.

By 6:30, he was sipping his favorite Bollinger Champagne

with Horatio sitting across from him. Nick reached over and they clinked glasses. They were in one of the many Michelin-starred restaurants in Lugano. The waiter knew Horatio and made suggestions for dinner, which they both ordered.

Two men in Horatio's security detail were at another table.

"Do you usually travel with a security team?" Nick asked.

"No. I usually take my security with me only when I am on assignment, otherwise, I travel alone. This is a special case since you were a target."

"I'm sorry about the damage to your cars," Nick said.

"Don't worry about it. It's time they were upgraded."

"That's the second time someone has told me that lately."

Nick looked across the restaurant at the two men. One was facing the front of the restaurant, and the other the rear. They were talking quietly, but were vigilant, scanning the room and the doors.

"How can I pay for your assistance?" Nick asked. "Perhaps we can do a trade for services?"

"Think nothing of it. I had a few free days. My team needs constant practice and training, and they like nothing better than an extraction. It had been more than a year since we had performed one. We will gather back in Gstaad and discuss how it went."

"I don't have any basis for comparison, but it was flawless to me."

"Yes, they did well," Horatio said. "Having a team nearby made all the difference."

"I'd like to do something nice for Massimo and Allegra," Nick said, taking a sip of champagne.

"You already have. I recommended them both to a friend who has an elite private car service I often use. Their income will probably double."

"That's good of you," Nick said.

"It's hard to find competent people with a calm demeanor who will do what it takes to ensure their client's safety."

Horatio leaned forward and picked up his glass. "John Mitchell filled me in on the details of the embezzlement by your business partner. Lance Grabowski is still in the wind?"

"I haven't asked Mitchell about him lately, but I assume he would tell me if he was spotted."

"Perhaps I can help with that," Horatio said.

"You can work with the FBI to help track down Lance?"

"I have other resources."

After dinner, Horatio returned to Gstaad and Nick returned to the hotel. It was early, and even though he was exhausted, he entered the lobby and took a seat at the bar. On the shelf in front of him was a bottle of Banqero Swiss rum. Nick didn't know there was a Swiss rum, and he ordered a glass from the busy bartender.

While he sipped, he thought about the twisted and curving path that took him to the *Hotel Gabbani* in Lugano. A strange connection of dots defined his course. He had always been open to new experiences, and life provided him with many. He never understood how people could let opportunities pass them by. Fear, he figured. He had to admit, this adventure took a hard, wrong turn.

FORTY-NINE
HEADING HOME

Nick slept a solid, dreamless sleep and awoke refreshed. The next morning, he took a bath and dressed. He found even in today's casual world, a blazer will open doors, and a suit and tie will get one through most obstacles, and dealing with obstacles was a large part of traveling.

Horatio had returned to Gstaad, and a taxi was waiting outside the hotel to give Nick a ride to the airport, and the Swissair flight back to Milan.

The short ride to the airport was an uneventful, yet blazingly fast one, and Nick had had enough high-speed driving for the trip.

"Vorrei andare alla aeroporto, non vada in orbita!" he told the driver. *I'd like to go to the airport, not into orbit!*

Willie's Italian sure came in handy on this trip, Nick thought. The driver rewarded him with a bark of laughter and a ten-kilometer-an-hour reduction in speed. A few moments later, they arrived at a skidding stop.

Nick got out and paid the pilot behind the controls, who flew off to the taxi line to await another launch.

Nick entered the airport terminal and started his trip back

home to Icarus nearly eight thousand miles away, looking forward to the relative calm of the unending parade of tourists and the noise and chaos of Honolulu.

After landing at Malpensa Airport in Milan, Nick made his way to the Alitalia counter.

"Yoo hoo," a voice called. Maddie waved Nick to their line.

"You are going to get out of Milan alive, I see," Geoff offered.

"I believe I will," Nick replied. *I guess twirling on the bull's testicles worked.*

"Everyone is talking about Luigi Donati's arrest. Was that your doing? Maddie asked.

"I may have been involved," Nick said, "Although I ask you to keep my name out of it, as I did with yours."

"Of course, I will," Maddie said.

"I've heard Mr. Donati surrounded himself with unsavory characters," Geoff added.

"You sure left a mark on this town. Good for you," Maddie said.

"Good for everyone," Geoff added.

Geoff and Maddie's flight was soon to depart, and Nick took a leisurely tour of the airport shop while he waited for his flight to be called.

On the plane, he settled in and introduced himself to his seatmate. Janet was an Italian-American flight attendant based in Newark. She had been touring Northern Italy with her mother.

"Did you enjoy your visit to Milan? What brought you here?" she asked.

Nick filled her in on the more interesting events of the past week.

"Wow. You really had a time of it."

"It was quite a carnival ride," he replied. "Until last night I had so little sleep, it felt like I had been experiencing a very long and contorted dream."

Nick and Janet drank champagne from a full bottle, compliments of one of the cabin crew, who knew Janet. When one of the flight attendants saw the ice bucket with a champagne bottle on Nick's tray, she watched them for a moment and then asked, "Are you on your honeymoon?"

Janet let out a laugh. "That would be nice, but no."

Nick turned to her. "Yes, that would be nice. I assume a wonderful woman like you is spoken for?"

"I am. I don't see a wedding ring. Do you have a girlfriend?" Janet asked.

Nick thought of Feral and then of Skye. "I met a woman I liked in Milan who lives in Paris. But that's a long way from Honolulu."

They flew over the Alps, Paris, London, and Greenland. The weather was clear and they could see icebergs out the window.

During the flight, the cabin crew addressed Nick in Italian. "*Un caffé o tè? Pollo o pàsta?*" He answered them in Italian.

When the cabin crew passed out the customs declaration, Nick asked, "May I have the U.S. form, please?"

The flight attendant stopped dead in her tracks, mouth hanging open.

"*Mi scusi.* Uh, what?" came the English with a Kiwi accent.

"May I please have the U.S. customs declaration form?" Nick asked again.

"Uh, I thought you were Swiss Italian," she said, handing him the correct form.

"I get that a lot."

Janet laughed.

When they were alone, Nick told her, "They had no idea of what to make of me. I fully enjoyed that novel experience."

"How did you find the Italians?" she asked.

"As a whole, I liked them. We fell into a bad crowd. They are in every corner of this round world."

"That's true where I came from," Janet said, taking a sip of champagne. "I would like to buy a tie for my boyfriend. I like the way you dress. Would you help me pick one out?"

"Thank you. Of course, I'll help. But he will risk looking like a Swiss banker."

The flight attendant brought samples, as they do on Alitalia. Nick chose a tie he would buy for himself.

Janet bought two of the same design and insisted that Nick have one.

Fourteen hours and a change of plane later, Nick was approaching the North Shore of Oahu. The plane made a wide turn toward the island of Kauai, then another turn until they were on final approach to Honolulu's reef runway. Out the window, the endless expanse of the blue Pacific was dotted with fishing and pleasure boats. Nick longed to get Icarus out on the water and clear his mind of the previous weeks.

Part Three
Honolulu

FIFTY
THE DRAGON UPSTAIRS

"I haven't been to this place in years," Willie said.

It was around 8:00 p.m., and Nick and Willie were in a tiny jazz and blues establishment called *The Dragon Upstairs* in Honolulu Chinatown.

To get to the club, one first found *Hank's Café* on Nu'uanu Street. Next door was a dilapidated green awning with the bar's name. Through the dragon painted on the door, you climbed the stairs, following a painted tail of a dragon until you reached its head at the top, opening up to a small room with a small stage and an even smaller bar. There were large, back-lit, colorful Asian masks on the walls.

Lester Young and Oscar Peterson's rendition of *I Can't Get Started* was played by a saxophone, guitar, and drums trio.

"I love this place," Willie said.

"Me, too."

"So, good trip?"

"It was eventful. Thank you for the use of the clothes and the Italian lessons. It all came in handy."

"Glad it worked out," Willie said. "So, you got to experience one of Horatio's extractions?"

"I did."

"How was it? I see you're not drinking alcohol, so it could not have been that exciting."

"I think I drank a year's worth of alcohol on that trip." Nick took a sip of soda water and bitters. "As for the extraction, I felt as though I was being chased by bulls."

"It saved you a trip to Pamplona."

Nick set down his glass. "Most of the time, I was on the phone with the Swiss and Italian authorities and John Mitchell in San Francisco. The last 25 kilometers were the excitement. If our driver, Massimo hadn't gotten a call from a friend telling him Luigi's guys were gunning for me and then had his cousin Allegra get me across the border to Switzerland, I might not be here talking with you."

Nick then gave him a broad brush of the events.

"Well, it's good to have you back," Willie said, clinking his beer glass on Nick's.

"Good to be here."

"You should be more careful who you travel with next time," Willie said.

Nick turned to Willie. "You made the introduction."

"Yeah, that's true. So tell me about Allegra."

"She is a fantastic driver and she has a boyfriend."

FIFTY-ONE

ARE YOU FREE FOR DINNER TONIGHT?

November arrived. Nick was reading the morning paper at a table in the wood-paneled alcove in the ARS café. Suzanne had returned from Paris the week before and had asked to meet. As she walked in the door, he stood and pulled out a chair for her.

"I ordered coffee for you. This place does pour-over and it takes a while," Nick said.

"Thank you." She sat in the chair across from him.

They looked at each other across the table.

"It's nice to see you got back safe," Nick said.

Suzanne cocked her head. "I received a call from John Mitchell at the FBI, and a local agent paid me a visit yesterday here in Honolulu."

"John Mitchell and I go back a bit."

"I gathered. He told me you were instrumental in closing down Luigi's operation in Milan, and that Luigi was about to export the girls we met. He also told me about a high-speed chase to Switzerland involving gunfire."

"It was exciting, I'll give you that."

The barista waved to Nick.

"What do you like in your coffee?" Nick asked.

"Black is fine."

Nick retrieved her coffee and another cup for himself and brought them back to the table.

Suzanne took a sip. "Wow, that's really good."

She set down her cup. "I am sorry I abandoned you in Milan. Luigi told me you were a very bad guy and showed me newspaper articles about embezzlement in San Francisco. Hearing that, and with Luigi's bizarre behavior, it was all too much, and I didn't feel safe."

"You have good instincts; I don't blame you for getting out of Milan," Nick said. "I suppose I would have done the same. It got you out of the line of fire, and that's a good thing."

"Line of fire. Sorry about that. I had no idea any of that would happen."

"How could you?"

Suzanne gazed out the window and sipped her coffee. She turned back to Nick.

"Who is Horatio Martín?" Suzanne asked.

"A friend. A friend with amazing resources it turns out."

"Agent Mitchell said he probably saved your life."

"Yes, I'm sure Mitchell is right about that."

Nick took a sip of coffee. He truly owed Horatio a huge debt of gratitude.

"Agent Mitchell also said Mr. Martín may have saved my life as well. How did he know I was going to Paris?"

"I asked him to look out for you, that Luigi was probably after you as well. I didn't know what to think when you disappeared," Nick said.

"Thank you for that. Martín's men met me at the airport and escorted me around Paris for a few days. It was a good thing, too. Luigi had sent somebody after me."

"Horatio has a first-rate team."

"Maybe you can get a message to him and thank him for me?"

"Sure. I can do that."

Suzanne put down her cup. "Fabio from FIG in Paris was here a couple of days ago. He tried to get Emma Bedford to work for his agency and break her contract with me."

"What a business," Nick said, shaking his head.

"Emma doesn't trust anyone else to manage her. I think a couple of visits from the FBI made her think twice. She asked if she could get modeling work with me without her mother involved."

"You should probably wait until Emma is eighteen and an adult and she can sign her own contract," Nick suggested.

"That would be next month."

They finished their coffee, both lost in their own thoughts. Suzanne looked at the time on her phone and stood, followed by Nick.

"I need to pick up my son from daycare," she said. "Thank you again for your help."

"You're quite welcome."

When Suzanne was gone, Nick gathered the coffee cups, returned them to the counter, and got a glass of water. The place was not busy; he had just sat and picked up the newspaper when his mobile phone rang.

"Nick Thomas," he answered.

"Hello Nicholas, are you free for dinner tonight?" the accented voice asked.

"Yes, I am, Skye. How are you?"

"I'm fine. I'm in Honolulu," she said.

"You are a long way from home. Are you here on business?"

"Uh, huh," she said noncommittally. "Can we dine at eight? I'll call you later and tell you where."

"That would be fine," he said.

"Okay, *Ciao*." She hung up.

Nick looked at his phone. *The woman does not believe in long goodbyes.*

He reached into his pocket and withdrew the piece of lapis lazuli Skye had handed him in the package at the party in Milan. He ran his finger across its polished surface.

He pondered what the weekend had in store for him. He shrugged and returned to the newspaper. There was an article about a transportation strike in France and how the country had come to a standstill. A photo showed the *Place de la Concorde* as a sea of parked cars. There, standing amid the stopped traffic, was their driver, Massimo.

Nick Thomas will return in

RADIO FREE LAKE PARADISO

Afterword

If you are a victim of human trafficking or suspect human trafficking is occurring and are in the United States, call the National Human Trafficking Hotline at 1-888-373-7888 or visit their website at

https://humantraffickinghotline.org

For more information on human trafficking worldwide, see the *Global Report on Trafficking in Persons* on the United Nations website.

https://www.unodc.org/unodc/en/human-trafficking/global-report-on-trafficking-in-persons.html

About the Author

Patrick Livanos Lester is a writer, artist, and gemologist. He worked with a team at NASA, designing a cockpit traffic display and collision avoidance system (TCAS) for aircraft. Later, he was a senior flight operations engineer on NASA's space station and shuttle programs and an international business consultant. He lives with his wife Kim in California, Hawaii, and other places with sailboats and palm trees.

Reviews are very important to authors. If you enjoyed *Nine Days in Milan*, please consider leaving a review. It would be greatly appreciated. All it takes is a sentence or two.

You can also send Patrick an email via the *Contact* tab at www.eastofhawaii.com. He will answer personally.

Check out the East of Hawaii website at www.eastofhawaii.com. It has book and music reviews, photos, and tidbits, relevant and not to his books. Sign up for Patrick's newsletter and receive the free e-book *Caviar Stories: A Short History of Caviar*.

EAST OF HAWAII

www.ingramcontent.com/pod-product-compliance
Lightning Source LLC
Chambersburg PA
CBHW051300210726
48287CB00002B/587